Greedy Little Thing

A Book of Desires Novel

Sonya Lawson

SauceBox Press

Copyright © 2025 by Sonya Lawson

All rights reserved.

No part of this publication may be reproduced, distributed, or transmitted in any form or by any means, including photocopying, recording, or other electronic or mechanical methods, without the prior written permission of the publisher, except as permitted by U.S. copyright law. For permission requests, contact SauceBox Press via sauceboxpress.com or Sonya Lawson at sonya@sonyalawson.com.

The story, all names, characters, and incidents portrayed in this production are fictitious. No identification with actual persons (living or deceased), places, buildings, and products is intended or should be inferred.

Book Cover by Gisele Giarola.

To all the poor girls, past and present. It's hard out here for those in it and those of us who somehow managed to claw our way out of it.

Know there are so many like you who are cheering you on every day.

This book contains scenes that may depict, mention, or discuss: academic mistreatment, anxiety, mistreatment at work/by a supervisor, and poverty.
Please take care of yourself as you read.

Contents

Chapter 1	1
Chapter 2	12
Chapter 3	21
Chapter 4	33
Chapter 5	45
Chapter 6	56
Chapter 7	70
Chapter 8	74
Chapter 9	87
Chapter 10	101
Chapter 11	112
Chapter 12	122
Chapter 13	131
Chapter 14	137
Chapter 15	151
Chapter 16	164

Chapter 17	173
Chapter 18	180
Chapter 19	188
Chapter 20	197
Want More?	203
About the Author	204
Acknowledgements	205

Chapter 1

"Edith..." Her full name slithered out into the world like a snake ready to strike, making her face scrunched in distaste.

A heavy hand tapped her arm and she shrugged it off, accidentally bumping the magnifying lenses into the incredibly old, incredibly rare book perched on her elevated workstation.

"Edith!" No snake slithering there, just plain old admonishment.

She sighed, pushed aside her desk-mounted magnifying glass and turned her pink-dyed head to face her boss. Technically he was her internship mentor, but he was unlike her academic mentors in the Library and Media Studies Department where she was completing her master's degree. They were at least earnest in their occupations and focus, if a little snooty or dismissive at times. They respected books first and foremost, maybe even at the expense of reality. It gave her some solid footing with them. Common ground she didn't usually have with the type of people who usually populated academia. Mitchel, however, held no common ground with her or the books she loved. He was concerned with spreadsheets and timecards and the "well-oiled machine," which was, regrettably, what he called the rare books section he managed in the private library and museum where E worked. A beautiful collection which grew constantly, but one he only saw as numbers.

Which was likely why he was there, looming over E, that very moment. Sadly, the LMS program was strapped. As was she. As she'd always been, coming from her small rural town's trailer park all the way to NYC as a graduate student. To offset her stipends, the program required paid internships. "Paid" was laughable, for the amount of work performed versus the amount listed on her direct deposits every month.

E was broke. No lies. Loans were tapped out for the year, and it was only June, meaning she had two more months of rent, bills, and food to somehow manage on only her intern dollars. Three, if she were honest, because she had to move after she graduated and sustain herself until her first paycheck. She couldn't get a second job. Besides the fact she'd had to sign a contract stating she'd not work anywhere else while in the LMS program, she was frantically finishing her thesis. Her eighteen-hour workdays went from the museum library to home or the university library where she researched, wrote, and edited.

In two months, she'd be free. Graduated and ready to take on the actual, factual, living-wage paying job she lined up for herself.

Didn't help her in the present, when bills piled up and her cupboards were nearly bare. Sure, she'd made this choice.

She hadn't gone into Library Sciences for money. No librarian made a lot of money, but they cared for books and people, a combination she loved. Loved since her early years, when she was far too young to furiously pedal her bike the four miles round trip to her local library and spend hours in the stacks, on the computers, chatting with all the librarians who watched her grow up. Watched her more closely than her parents could at times, what with the number of hours they had to work at their minimum-wage jobs to stay afloat, even in a trailer park.

No, she wasn't in for a life of wealth. Wealth wasn't what she needed. She needed good work, meaningful work, helping people and preserving book history. She also needed to eat and keep her lights on, which meant she needed to suck it up and have a conversation with Mitchel.

Mitchel craned his neck over her head, wrinkling his nose as he did. "Are you still on the York manuscript, Edith?"

E bit her tongue, as she did so often with him. He refused to call her E, her preferred name. Instead, he called her Edith, which was technically her name, but still, decent people took into account what others preferred.

She nodded. What could she say? The manuscript was a bound collection of broadsheets detailing the Siege of York during the English Civil War. An interesting piece filled with numerous documents of historical significance. Her job was to catalogue, report, and carefully release each from the four-hundred-year-old binding. A tedious process, as Mitchel knew. So why he questioned her still being on it when she received the assignment only four days ago was a mystery. But a lot in life mystified E, so she simply chose to not engage.

He sniffed, tugged his immaculate and likely expensive shirt sleeve down under his impeccable navy jacket and looked into E's eyes. She knew what he saw: pink dyed hair to her shoulders, copper-brown eyes, a too bulbous nose on an otherwise small face, and an average, though short, body wrapped in a thrift store button up and slacks, which were clean and tidy but threadbare around certain seams. He didn't like any of it. Fine with E. She wasn't there to impress him with her looks. She was there to do a good job and complete her internship for her degree, which she did magnificently, in her opinion.

Her mind back on track, she squared her shoulders and looked Mitchel in his mud-brown eyes, which happened to be almost level with her own. Possibly one reason his attitude was bad: he chose Napoleon complex over short king energy.

"Did you receive my message, Mitchel?"

"Yes," he said, leaning to her side to straighten a metal ruler on her desk. "What do you wish to discuss?"

E looked around the room. She shared a workspace with three others who worked full-time in the book preservation department. They were all studiously ignoring the two talking in the quiet space, but they could hear every word. "Could we talk in your office?"

Mitchel let out a sigh as if the request ruined his entire life before he spun on his heels. "Come," he called to her, not even bothering to look over his shoulder at her. It grated more than a bit, but she followed, because what else could she do? She needed to eat, and this man might as well hold the keys to her refrigerator.

She settled into the artfully worn brown leather chair in Mitchel's office. The walls were a deep burgundy, the chairs all leather, and the lights were absurdly dim for someone who worked on, or at least with, books.

Mitchel leaned forward at his desk, placing his elbows on the gleaming wooden surface, lacing his fingers together before cocking his head her way. "Again, what do you wish to discuss, Edith?"

"Well, Mitchel, I was wondering if there was any wiggle room in the intern budget."

At the mention of money, Mitchel's back went ramrod straight. He was notoriously tight-fisted, which was why he used interns whenever and wherever he could. Likely also why he rose in the ranks so quickly. He was better at budgets than books, from what E saw, and libraries needed a bit of both to run smoothly. She recognized that, but it didn't mean she appreciated Mitchel and his ways.

"Now, Edith. Your internship compensation was negotiated months ago, with your department. If you have an issue with your compensation, you really should speak with them."

An exasperated sound leaked out before she could trap it. "I did. Yesterday. Which is why I emailed you for a meeting today. They say they can't do anything about the compensation package offered by an institution outside the university. That's all you."

Mitchel leaned back in his chair, looking down at his neat and tidy desk for a beat before meeting her eyes again. "Edith, you signed a contract."

"I know, Mitchel." Stating the obvious didn't help the situation. E decided to swallow the lump in her throat and be honest with the man. "I can't keep up with my work and my bills right now. I need a little more to get by until the end of this internship. I'm not looking for a huge raise, Mitchel. Even a dollar more an hour would help."

He looked puzzled. "Why not ask your family for assistance if it's only for a short time?"

E instantly went rigid, rage and a hint of bitterness coursing through her veins at the question. The department chair had asked the same thing yesterday. It was infuriating. One, she did the same type and amount of work as the full-time employees here, and she was paid a fraction of what they made. Two, the assumption she came from a family who could help her financially, even briefly, always grated. Most in academia or in careers fed by academia had this attitude. Mainly because it was the case for centuries, she supposed, but it was the twenty-first century. Assuming people came from money was absurd. She rarely even got a chance to talk to her parents because they worked so much. She visited them once a year, if she could, because none of them could afford the price of a plane ticket without planning and saving. Her parents barely made rent and bills on their own old-ass trailer in Ohio. No way they were helping her with money.

"No," she bit out without explanation.

"Loans?" he asked.

"Tapped out." She couldn't get any more this year. Maybe she could get a private student loan, but that was asking for more financial disasters down the road, what with the debt she now had.

She'd been lucky in one regard. She'd had a full ride scholarship to Ohio State, which she happily took. She had the same from the NYU grad school. She'd worked enough, saved enough, all through high school and undergrad, to pay her own bills. Until she came to the city. Until she tried to do something to help drag herself out of the cycle of poverty by using her head instead of her hands. She worked her ass off in school for her stipend, worked hard every day at this internship, but the reality of the world was she worked and worked and worked, and every day, her savings dwindled down lower and lower.

She'd had to take out her first student loan at the beginning of the year. Took all they'd give her after they deducted her stipend, her scholarships, everything else they gave her in her financial aid package. It was enough to cover necessities for a year. Then, her roommate, who owned the apartment she lived in thanks to a generous gift from her parents, left for an internship at the British Library. E was happy for Lisa, but it meant she had to take on all the bills instead of just half. Okay, so technically she didn't have to take it all on herself.

Lisa had offered to keep their arrangement as it was, but she already paid so little in rent it was bordering on charity. The least she could do was pay all the monthly bills for the place while Lisa wasn't even living there.

Lisa didn't have to worry about such things, as her parents were paying for her flat in London while she lived there. No shade to Lisa, but it made E jealous when she thought about it too long. And she loved Lisa, so she tried not to think about it too much.

E wanted to make her own way in the world, like she knew she'd be able to in a few short months. She was all set to move back to Columbus, return to the Special Collections Library at Ohio State where she'd had a work study position as an undergrad. This time, though, she'd do it with a respectable Midwestern salary. She'd never be rich, sure, but she'd never want like she had growing up, either. It was a step up for her. If only she could get there. And she was trying like hell to get there, which included having this demeaning conversation with her uppity boss.

"Well, Edith, I'm afraid there's nothing I can do. My budget for the quarter was set months ago, the money already allocated. I have no additional funds to give you." He shrugged at her, as if it were nothing. As if money wasn't a very real, very pressing concern. As if he'd never known hard times, and E figured he probably hadn't. Not with his manners and his dress and his flippant question earlier. He'd never understand what it was to live on bologna and crackers for a week because there was nothing else.

She fisted her hands, digging her nails into her palms to help her fight back the tears creeping up her throat. "Very well," she said, rising to leave. With her back to him, her hand on the doorknob, he stopped her.

"Edith, if I could..." He let the sentence drop.

Good thing, because anything he said after those four words would've been a lie. They both knew it. She nodded, more to shake out her head than to acknowledge his words, and left, her hopes of surviving two more months in the city on her own steam no more than dust on Mitchel's lush Persian rug.

E went to the bathroom to gather herself and then went back to work. No one would ever say she didn't work hard, didn't do what was asked of her, even when she suffered. She meticulously reported, catalogued, and unbound for six more hours, letting the history in her hands and delicacy of her job force out the cacophony of worry in her mind. Mostly.

She did think on it some. Couldn't help it. The worry over money was constant background noise in her head. Always had been and might always be. At one point she caught herself in the middle of a brood, thinking about all she wanted, all others had that she didn't have, and the unfairness of it all. She gripped a metal ruler so tightly it left harsh red lines in her palm. She might have not noticed it if a bustle across the room hadn't brought her out of the worry trance.

Anne, one of her more vocal and friendly co-workers, was frantically searching for something over at her workstation. She specialized in medieval texts, and she was counting and recounting a small stack of books. "It was just here," she said. The soft words dropped like a mallet in the quiet room.

"Anne, you okay?" E asked.

"No. I'm going bonkers. I could've sworn Mitchel brought me three new books to review, these two Latin manuscripts and a Latin and Middle English text. I hadn't even really looked at it when he put the stack here, but the Middle English stood out. I rarely see those here. And it looked like it could be a spell-book, which would be an impressive find. Now, I can't find it anywhere."

E moved over to the woman, scanning the small room and other workstations as she did. "Did he come pick it back up? Maybe it got requested by a researcher. Let's check the log."

"Yeesh. I hope the log isn't being wonky again." The week before, their Romance language expert, Brian, had expressed some concern about a few books missing from the database. Mitchel waved away the concern, saying it was likely a bug in the system, but it made everyone a little wary. There were even mutters of wishing card catalogues were still a thing, which, fair enough.

E bumped Anne's shoulder and called her over to her workstation laptop. She balanced it on her knee, as there was no room on her desk with her own manuscript in pieces there, but she managed to pull up the official log on their employee site. It showed what each person was assigned at any given time. Anne's name popped up after E's search, and there on the screen were two new Latin titles. Exactly what was on her station. No Middle English with Latin book in sight.

"This is still wonky, or I'm going cuckoo," the middle-aged woman said, tightening her cashmere cardigan around herself. "I swear I saw..."

"It's okay, Anne," E said, patting her shoulder in comfort. An awkward, rusty gesture, but one, nonetheless. "All that Latin muddles the brain."

Anne laughed, the sound cracking through the room.

"No, seriously. Mitchel probably just reassigned it." Anne bit her lip but thanked E before she shuffled back to her own station and silence again fell over the space.

E thought nothing of the missing book or glitching database as she worked. Didn't think about it as she carefully packed away her unfinished tasks at closing time. Not a thought of it when she slung her messenger bag on, and it felt a smidge heftier than it should.

She took the subway all the way from Madison to her third-floor apartment on 8th. It was one-bedroom but had a small, exposed brick alcove big enough for a double bed, bookcase, and desk, which is where she stayed, even with Lisa out of the country. It was Lisa's apartment; E wouldn't take Lisa's room even if she was gone.

She threw her bag on her bed, unzipped it to get out a notebook, but pulled out a slim, cracked leather book instead. Latin shone in gilded print on the spine and cover. E knew enough Latin to decipher this title. Knew it from the words and the odd tingle creeping down her spine at what she saw. *Liber Desideriorum* it read. *The Book of Desires*.

Chapter 2

E was on her third big glass of her Two Buck Chuck wine. Sadly, the chuck wasn't even two bucks anymore, so she'd been saving this bottle for an opportune time. A time like right then, when wallowing seemed like the best option. She gulped the dregs of the serviceable cabernet in her glass and reached for the bottle on the coffee table. Sitting cross-legged on the small, fluffy couch in the middle of the living room made it somewhat difficult, so she ended up toppling forward, smacking one hand down on the coffee table as her head careened toward it. A yelp, then a harsh laugh ripped through the small apartment as she corrected her position and gave herself a figurative pat on the back for managing to save her head and her wineglass at the same time.

"Maybe I don't need this," she muttered as she stood with the wineglass in one hand and the nearly empty bottle in the other. Feeling sorry for herself wasn't new to E, but it also wasn't a habit. She had a shitty life at times, and wallowing felt good when it got shittier. Knowing she'd dust herself off in the morning and get to work figuring out how to survive for two months made it not feel nearly as pathetic.

Maybe she could get a new credit card and max it out? Deal with the consequences later. She already had a solid chunk of debt to deal with thanks to two years in NYC, so why the hell not? Gritting her teeth, she imagined big, cartoony bags of money labeled "debt" in her head, with a tiny cartoon her being squashed by all of them.

"Fuck it," she said, either to the debt or the wine, because she brought the bottle to her lips, and in a few strong pulls, finished it off. Her balance faltered as she threw her head back, making her stumble. Maybe it was a good thing she had no more wine in the place, she thought. She'd obviously had enough. Not drunk, but not exactly sober, for sure. "Thanks, grad school," she said with a mock salute of the empty, red-stained wine glass in her hand to the equally empty room at large. It was true that college and grad school gave her a slightly higher alcohol tolerance over the years, which helped when she wanted to drown her sorrows but didn't want to go overboard. Then again, it didn't make her a cheap date any longer either, and she needed to pinch where she could.

Her feet and legs were heavy, unwieldy, but not completely unmanageable. She bent to put the wineglass in the sink for later, right beside her one, lonely dirty fork and the red-stained Tupperware which had held her dinner leftovers. Cheap pasta, canned sauce, and powdered parmesan went a long way for someone on a budget, and she'd managed to stretch it out over four days of dinners that week. A snort escaped when she thought about what Mitchel might have had for dinner that evening. Expensive sushi, maybe. Or a nice dry-aged steak at a frou-frou place like Delmonico's. E only knew about Delmonico's because Lisa's parents had taken her with them for a celebration dinner when they'd both gotten internships at their top choices, a once in a lifetime treat for someone like her.

With a combo of anger and sadness and self-pity welling up inside, she tossed the wine bottle into the recycling, her shoulders bunching when she heard the deep clatter and bang of the heavy glass hitting the bin. At least the tinkling of broken glass didn't sound, so she shrugged it off and moved with slow, plodding steps toward her alcove.

Lisa was gone, had been for months at this point, and E had the apartment all to herself. Despite this, she still pulled her makeshift privacy curtain tight against the city lights outside the living room windows. A small, muted grayscale world of bed, desk, and bookcase spread before her. Her clothes, hanging above her bookcase thanks to the box store rack and shelf system she installed when she first moved in, swayed slightly when she disturbed the air. She had little there; everything in similar colors and styles to easily mix and match. Lisa had talked about how smart capsule wardrobes were when she'd first seen it, which made E's face flame with shame. She wasn't trendy, just poor. Something Lisa, bless her kind soul, didn't know anything about.

She burrowed into the oversized t-shirt she'd won at a trivia night in college and the red-and-black pajama bottoms she'd had since high school. One good thing about keeping clothes for an absurdly long amount of time: threadbare t-shirts and flannel pants were comfier than new. She crawled into her bed, which thanks to Lisa once again, was comfy. Her friend had bought the thing, claiming she'd wanted it to keep for guests at some point. It hugged her like a cloud, warm and loving and making her miss Lisa, who would have drunk the bottle of wine with her, uncorked a second, and railed about the unfairness of it all, even when she couldn't fully comprehend what it meant or how it felt.

E moved to get under the comforter, her leg slipping a bit and bumping her bag. She muttered to herself as she hefted it off the bed and placed it on the old wooden chair at her desk. A thump sounded behind her, and she whirled, staring a moment at the slim book she'd found earlier. E could've sworn she placed the thing on her desk, not back on her bed, fully intending to get it back to work somehow without anyone noticing. She definitely didn't need people thinking she'd stolen it. Mitchel might be more wary of her intentions when it came to such things. Rich people often were when they found out someone they knew was poor. But, in all honesty, with her looks and clothes and general demeanor, he probably knew how poor she was long ago.

Her head was hazy, running through such weird, paranoid thoughts as she stood staring down at the small book. The thing shimmered against the hardwood floor, as if it emanated its own light. Ridiculous, she knew, so she scooped it up to place it on her desk. But now, with lots of wine in her system, she was intrigued. E turned, taking the two whole steps back to her bed and laying down across the width, her upper body rested but her feet still planted on the floor.

Holding the book up over her head, she flipped through the pages, the scent of old paper and binding smacking her in the face. E breathed the smell she loved deep, happy to have it here when she was feeling so down about her life, her choices, her options. This book was like all the ones she'd helped over the years; all the books she could potentially bring new life to one day. If she just got through these bare days.

"I will, damnit. But money'd sure make it a helluva lot easier," she muttered to herself. The book slipped from her grip, crashing down on her face. "Shit!" She yelped, rubbing her now-sore nose as she sat up in bed. Her hand held the book open to a beautiful page. E blinked up at it, noting the gold and green filigree that appeared remarkably preserved, even to her tipsy eyes. At the top, in the squared but elegant medieval script so often used in books from this period, was an oddity. The Middle English title read "To Somne Moneye for to Multiplie." She didn't know much Middle English, but this was close enough to modern English she got the gist.

Shooting upright in bed, she pulled the book close to her face, skimming the lines beneath the title. It was Latin. She got some of it. The first bit talked about gods and monsters and whatever else. The rest, though? It read like a spell. Damn, Anne'd been right.

She'd encountered a few spell books in her work. They were rare, because witches kept their books to themselves, passed down from witch to witch within a particular coven. Even though witches were known for writing a lot of things down, something other supernaturals like vampire and werewolves didn't exactly do, it stayed within their group. Much like all supernatural things, they stayed within their own clusters. Hell, E didn't blame them, what with their bloody history with humans. She'd met more supernaturals in NYC than she had in

Ohio. A handful of vampires and witches. They were cordial, if aloof, so she knew the basics of each group, but that was it.

Now even more fascinated, E flipped the book over in her hand, looking at the binding and title again. From the little she knew of spell books, it was abnormal for one to be written in both Middle English and Latin. Latin seemed to be the given, although she'd heard tell of older tomes in Greek and Egyptian hieroglyphs. Didn't matter much, because the coven usually included their own translations and notes and such. Which was why they rarely were found outside covens. They held too much knowledge and history to be forgotten or discarded. Hell, even the purges after the supernaturals revealed themselves to humans didn't mean any passed down to human museums or libraries. When they burned a witch, they burned all her books, too. Those types of humans always took the books along with the people, or even took the books before they started taking the people.

She huffed at the thought of how horrible people could be, but continued considering the book, turning it over in her hands while keeping her place with one finger. E wondered what, if anything, it could do for her. Or, maybe more aptly, what, if anything, she had to lose in trying something that had literally smacked her in the face.

E wasn't a witch. Had no witch blood in her family tree—that she knew of anyway. Every human knew only witches could use magic. It was the fundamental difference between witches and humans. Same with werewolves being able to change shape during the full moon phases. Same with vampires feeding only on blood. However, she was drunk enough to give the spell a whirl, despite knowing she was a basic human.

She felt stupid, but she continued anyway. The couch and coffee table were pushed back to give her a small open space on the hardwood floor. She'd grabbed the box of chalk she still had from her stint as a TA and made the circle described in the Latin bits of the spell. There were no visuals, so she could only hope she drew it right.

If money popped up in the middle of the circle, smack where all the intricate lines intersected, she'd maybe have to keep the book for herself. If it didn't, she'd simply wash the floor and go to bed a little more sober than she'd been when she'd crawled in there earlier.

Regardless, she was doing this thing, so she crossed her legs, pushed her shoulders back, rolled her neck for a second, and then scrunched back down into her reading posture. The book was full of spells. She'd gathered as much with a cursory look at the rest of the pages. Spells to get things or summon things. Whatever the caster desired, she supposed. Hence the name. She desired money, something to make her life easier, so that's the spell she'd use.

Blowing out a deep breath and taking in the smell of the book as she breathed deep once again, she started the process. First, she lit a candle. There weren't any cool, magic candles around. Not even the regular white tapered kind. So she lit the fat three-wick candle that smelled like clean laundry Lisa kept in the living room and called it good. Next, she closed the circle with the chalk, saying the incantation as she did, pulling on all her haphazard Latin and winging it with the Middle English as she went.

E stared at the center of the circle hard, so hard her eyes watered. Or maybe she simply cried. Nothing happened. As nothing ever happened. A minute passed, and she slammed the book closed a little too aggressively for something so old. She scooted back to get up to get a sponge and clean up the chalk mess, when a rumble sounded.

E turned her head this way and that, looking for the source. They didn't live close enough to the subway to get that rumble on the regular, so it had to be something else. Then, a small green light appeared, hovering mere inches above the center of the chalk outline. The light pulsed, growing wider and wider as she watched in awe. It pushed down to the floor, spreading out like tendrils when it hit the hardwood, growing to fill the circle but not spill out of its confines.

A flash of bright green blinded E, and she shielded her eyes. Blinking them to clear the flashing circles lingering there, she first noticed the feet. Like primate feet but deadlier, the tips like metallic blades at least an inch long. Gold-dusted skin stretched over taut muscles and veins. Feet made to grip like hands, each toe tipped with a hard gold claw. Wicked sharp and gleaming.

There was no money. No gold. But something else she'd summoned. Still cross-legged on the ground, only half a foot from the circle, she brought her eyes up, up, up, taking in the creature looming over her with rising fear.

The feet were bare, but the creature wore a gleaming white toga made from the shiniest silk she'd ever seen. Its clawed feet went up into strongly muscled calves and thighs before the silk covering him from mid-thigh up, laid across one shoulder on his chest where a large gold and ruby broach, oddly in the shape of a baby, clamped it all together. His forearms and biceps were a match for the impressive leg muscles, and from what she saw of it, the rest of his body: toned and fit. His skin was a light tan color, but with a golden sheen overlaying it.

When her eyes finally met his face, she gasped. Partly because he was all masculine beauty: Greek nose with high cheek bones, full lips, and startlingly green eyes. Partly because golden horns curved up from his head, rising above thick, close-cropped hair the color and shine of fresh-cut onyx. And his mouth, pulled back in a snarl, was filled with bright white teeth – including massive fangs, at least an inch long and sharpened to a glistening point, protruding from his mouth. He unfisted his hands at his sides and she noticed them for the first time, as beautiful and dangerous and clawed as his feet.

E scrambled back from the circle, unable to get her feet under her, scrambling so she inadvertently smudged a few inches of the chalk circle away. A pop sounded in the space, like a deep atmospheric switch, and the beast moved forward, quick as lightning, muscles bunching and shifting like a big cat about to pounce. E's feet slipped on the polished hardwood as she tried to get up, causing her to drop fast and hard right on her butt. She let out a yelp right as the clawed monster lunged for her.

Chapter 3

E spun on her butt to flee, to get away from the flash of teeth and claws bearing down on her. She didn't make it far. In fact, she hadn't even been able to turn away when the monster's massive hand gripped her throat. He lifted her up with one hand, though his grip wasn't hard enough to choke her. Not yet at least. She still scratched at his hand with her own, kicked out as best she could, but it did nothing. He brought her up to meet his face, dangling her off the ground as he did so, given their foot-and-a-half height difference. He shoved her back, back, back, until she hit the wall and slid down it to her feet. His face followed her as she went.

His snarl was all she heard, his fangs all she saw. The knife-like claws on his hands pressed in, cutting off air, digging into the flesh at the back of her neck but not quite cutting into her flesh. Before she couldn't breathe, however, she had breathed him in. It was an oddly pleasant scent, given everything else about the creature made her want to shrink away in fear. He smelled of tarnished metal, smoke, and whiskey. She thought of luxurious candles, dark wooden rooms where she'd never been, vaults of old jewelry she'd never seen in real life. More than this, however, the scent alone made her heart calm to manageable beats. Terror ran riot through E's mind, though a soft tingle started in her gut, pushing out the fear in the rest of her body for some reason.

The monster growled deep and low in his throat as dripping fangs grazed her neck. He audibly breathed in, noticeably froze for a second, then pulled back to study her face. He loosened his grip, so she could once again suck in air, which she did in big gulps. He said something she couldn't understand. Something in a language she didn't know but one which sounded familiar enough she knew it was human at least.

"I...I don't understand." Her voice was croaking, harsh because of the claws gripping her neck.

One second she was tipsy, trying to summon wealth to help her solve her problems, then the next this creature was on top of her. She did, somehow, understand the smell now. Not in a logical sense, but in her bones. The smell was significant, comforting, like a home she'd never known.

"English," the creature muttered. His tongue, long and pointed and oddly flexible, curled around one of his fangs as he gave her a smirk. He loosened his grip more, his hand coming to rest like a necklace at the base of her throat, and he leaned in again. She flinched out of reflex and general uncertainty, but all the monster did was breathe deep once again, his eyes fluttering closed before he blinked them back open. "Name," he said, his deep, dark voice a combination of promised pain and pleasure, an audible charge zipping from her ears down her spine until it hit her core and made her flutter.

She tamped that down real quick. Lust was something she did not need when some unknown creature from some unknown world had his hand around her throat, even if similar scenarios featured in alone-time fantasies.

"Edith. E, actually."

"E?" The question rang clear. He wanted more from her.

"E Michaels. From Middletown, Ohio. And... and you are?"

She told herself her engrained Midwestern manners compelled her to ask his name. She also could be honest with herself and admit it might also be the alluring smell of him. Or the sear of his body pushed against her own. All good options for the basic, "What's your name? Where're you from?" routine.

"Plutus," he said, pulling himself back at last. He released her neck and she moved to run, get away, but before she could, he slammed a hand into the exposed brick at her back. She heard a crunch, felt bits of brick dust fall to her shoulder. She knew, without having to look, there'd be a massive hand-shaped dent in Lisa's beautiful, exposed brick feature wall. The cost of fixing something like that drifted across her mind, but she locked it down, focusing on her current precarious situation, and any possibility she might have of surviving this encounter.

Plutus, the creature in front of her, had taken a moment to look around the apartment, surveying it. His eyes, a green so bright she thought they might be able to hypnotize, homed back in on her, studying her face once again. A frown touched his lips as he stared unblinking. A stray flash of light from the street caused his eyes to reflect red, then green, like a cat.

"You are human. How did you call me?"

"I didn't call you."

Plutus looked to the floor with the spell materials on the floor, his hand flexing then loosening more when he studied something there. "The book," he whispered. Slowly turning his head back to E, he looked her up and down, assessing, and she felt the need to fill the silence with some explanation.

"Well, what I mean is, I didn't intentionally call you. Specifically. I didn't think the spell would work, you know? Because, like you said, I'm human and all. I just needed..." E turned her head away from the monster, unintentionally exposing her neck to him, but she didn't care. The embarrassment of what she'd done, the desperation touching every corner of her life, made it impossible for her to tell him exactly what happened.

One too-pointy, gold-tipped claw flicked under her chin, making her eyes widen. He nudged her face back, so she looked in his eyes once again. "I see," was all he said. He nodded and took a step back, releasing his hand from the brick and her chin, giving her space she needed. However, she felt his eyes like a touch when they moved down to her feet and climbed back up her body, taking in all she was, which in her opinion wasn't much.

"Are we in Ohio?"

"No. Uh, this is New York. City."

He smiled wide then, his mouth transforming into something sharp and dirty and lovely all at once. He looked damn sexy, despite his horns and fangs and claws and the barely leashed power radiating off him. Something about Plutus called to her, scraped against her desire, and she wasn't too happy about it. Still, she wasn't one to ignore the obvious, so she could at least acknowledge a spark of want existed in her when she looked at him. Smelled him.

"Almost like home." His voice, smooth, held an odd accent she couldn't place. Old world somehow. Old money even. Something she never knew.

She blinked. Hard. Couldn't hold back the question any longer, though it maybe came out a bit ruder than she intended. "What are you?"

"Plutus. A god of wealth. The Greek God of Wealth, to be exact."

"A god?" she whispered, in pure disbelief. Sure, all humans knew about supernaturals, but they made up three distinct categories: witches, werewolves, or vampires. No one talked of gods, unless they were in a church. Or a mythology class. This dude in front of her—all six-and-a-half feet of muscle and power and sexy vibes—sure as hell wasn't myth.

He waved a hand in a dismissive way, still studying his surroundings. "Yes. God. Surprise! Gods exist. You should get used to the fact."

"Because you're in my apartment?"

"And I plan to stay," he said, the wicked smirk stretching back over his mouth.

The god turned, to take in more of the apartment, his eyes falling on the small bits of luxury she used every day that weren't hers. "A lovely home you have here. Makes me wonder why you'd attempt to call a being like me."

She straightened, wanting to defend herself. "First off, I didn't call a being of any kind. I called, um, well, money or something."

He barked out a laugh. "Or something? You're unsure," He tsked at her. "You really shouldn't try to cast spells you don't fully understand. You might bite off more than you can chew."

She ignored the very good advice he gave her a little too late and went on. "Second: this place isn't mine. My friend, Lisa, owns it. I stay here at a steep discount."

The smirk washed away and his head turned, right to her small alcove-made-bedroom. She felt something ugly move in her, and she pushed past him, for the first time truly unafraid, to rip the curtain open so he could see all her space. "Happy?" E asked, standing to face him with arms crossed and hip jutted.

He nodded, as if he'd decided something, and instead of answering, moved to sit on the misplaced couch. "Come," he said as he patted the couch cushion beside himself, his tone a clear indication he was used to being obeyed.

She didn't move. The more time she spent with him, the more she felt his scent seep into her, making her calm and admittedly feistier than she should be in this situation. Annoyance apparently overrode any lingering fear. E didn't move. Didn't come as he asked. She stood and stared, hard, and waited.

He sighed deep, the sound a mix of delight and exasperation, and leaned back, making himself more comfortable. "I can make you come." The words curled from his forked tongue, past his fangs, hitting her hard in her gut. She knew from the glint in his eyes he meant what he said in multiple ways. Still, she stood strong.

"Very well," he said, then he moved. Or she assumed he moved. One second he was sitting on the couch, and the next he was in front of her, gripping her waist and hoisting her up as if she weighed no more than a backpack. He slung her over his shoulder, and then the room blurred and she was bouncing, hard but safe, on the couch.

"Much better," he practically purred, sitting beside her. Plutus threw his left arm over the back of the couch and scooted close, turning in the seat so he faced her. She did the same, giving up her annoyance in favor of what she thought would come next: answers.

"Now, dear E, you called me to you. Whether you intended to do so or not, you used *The Book of Desires,* and I appeared. That's what happened, yes?"

E nodded, giving him no more, waiting to see what he'd say.

"Good. Now, as the god of wealth, I can do much for you." His massive clawed right hand landed softly on her pajama-clad thigh. It was big enough he could grip it all the way around in one hand if he wished. He squeezed lightly, to emphasize what he was about to say.

"I can give you your every desire. You want wealth, correct?"

She squirmed then, thinking of the desires creeping through her that had nothing to do with money, but she did answer him. "Not wealth. I'm not greedy. I just— I want to be comfortable. I want the ability to live life and not worry about money all the damn time."

"E," he said softly, "Wealth is the only thing which can do this, and even this can't make a person live life worry-free."

"I know." She didn't, not really. E had never known a life where a worry about money wasn't the same as worry over survival. Intellectually, she understood worries came and went for everyone, money or not. She just needed a break. "I want to live, not survive. Or barely survive."

"Very well," he said, loosening his grip on her thigh to pat it again. "I can give it to you. For a price."

"Price."

"Of course, E. I'm a businessman of sorts. Have been for many, many centuries." He leaned close, his breath whispering over her ear when he breathed out. "I don't do anything for free, little one."

She shook her head to dislodge his intoxicating smell and leaned farther away from him, eyebrows cocked and eyes narrowed in skepticism. "What's the cost?" She knew about devil's bargains. She'd read "The Monkey's Paw." Wording mattered, so she needed to be clear.

His brilliant green eyes squinted, drilling into her own, as if he could look upon her soul, evaluate the highest price he could extract. Then, with a wicked smile, he said, "Time."

"'Time' is vague, Plutus. Be more specific."

"Specifically, I require one month of your time. Full access to you for four weeks."

"What does full access entail?"

A grin crept over his face, revealing the tips of his fangs. "You spend your days and nights by my side. Anything else,"—he winked at her, and she flushed— "would be outside the purview of any bargain. Given of your own free will and with enthusiastic consent."

"Okay. You require me to spend four weeks with you, day and night. For this, you'll give me wealth. But what do you mean by wealth?"

"You want to not worry about survival. I can do that. At the end of our time, you'll be left with enough funds, in whatever form you choose, to live your life and never again have worry about monetary survival."

"I have work." E didn't like who she worked for, but she liked her work. Plus, she hadn't not worked since she was fifteen. Earlier if you counted babysitting and such. She'd feel weird not working. She also had research to do to finish her thesis. Her days were packed as is, so she didn't know how much time she could give the guy, god or no.

"I can handle that for you" he said, his tone blasé.

"I don't want you to handle it," she countered, heat seeping into her voice. "I enjoy my work. I also have school, which is another type of work, and I will not give that up. Both are important to me."

"I can allow you time to do what you must, E. However, this is a bargain. A verbal contract. If you want the reward you must commit to the terms."

She bit her lip, thinking hard on the issue. "I can't give up my research time, but if it were somehow possible, I could give up some of the time spent at my internship. A big if, however. It'd need to not count against me in my degree program, I'd still need my paycheck to be the same, and it'd need to not negatively affect my coworkers there."

"All doable. Agreed." He said, sliding closer, a feat she didn't think was possible a second before.

The thrill of the promise coursed through her. She went over his words in her head, thinking about any tricks he might be able to pull, then came to a decision. "Yes," she said, clear and strong. "I agree to your terms."

"Let's seal it, then," he said, leaning in swiftly to take her mouth in a hard, quick kiss. A spark of something, like a live electric current, zapped through E. In its wake, something burned, twined in her gut. She couldn't see it, but a hidden part of her brain told her something bound them together.

"Great," Plutus said, clapping his hands hard and rising from the couch. "We start tonight. Let's go."

"Tonight?" E looked down at her pajamas. She'd much rather cuddle on the couch than go anywhere. "Where are we going?"

"The night is young, little one," he said, reaching down to run a claw gently down her cheek. "Where do you go to celebrate?"

She wasn't a celebrater. Had little to celebrate in her time, and little funds to do it with even when she should celebrate. The only thing that came to mind she said. "A nightclub."

Plutus straightened and cut her a hard look. "What do you do in nightclubs?"

"Do you not know what a nightclub is?"

He laughed. "Of course I know what a nightclub is. I've even invested in a few. I want to know what *you* do in a nightclub."

She'd only been to a few in NYC, because all the good ones took too much money. And she did prefer to hang with a few people than a crowd. What she did was more theoretical than not.

Picking herself up off the couch, she answered. "Dance. Drink. Watch people show off or show out."

"Show off?"

"Depends on the club. And before you ask, I only know of a few. One of which is more upscale."

E'd been to Paradise once, and only because Lisa had dragged her there a week before she left for London as a last hurrah. Lisa knew the owner, had gone to private school in Connecticut with him or something. It's the only way they'd gotten in, or, at least, the only way E would've ever gotten in to such a place.

The thought made her pause. "Plutus, fancier night clubs can be hard to get into."

He snorted as if her words were funny. "No need to worry, E. No need to worry any longer, as I promised. No door to luxury or wealth is ever closed to me."

He stepped closer, looked down at her pajamas and said, softly, "Would you like to change into something..."

"Yes. Of course." She scrambled back to her alcove, staring at her meager closet and her lack of club attire.

"You need a dress," Plutus said. Not a question, but a statement.

She spun toward him and nodded, not being able to voice the need as she wrung her hands together. He looked down at her, watched her hands for a moment, his jaw tightening. Without warning, a dress appeared in his hands. It poured down as he held it up to her: a shimmering sheath of rose gold silk with small cap sleeves and a deep v neckline. It looked slightly art deco, a little flapper. It was breathtaking in its beauty. A work of art in dress form.

She didn't move to take it, hesitant to put something so lux in her hands, so Plutus met her instead. He pushed the silk into her body, holding it up to her as if judging its fit. He looked up into her eyes. "Perfection."

She caught the thing when he let it go, the idea of it hitting the floor overriding all her hesitations.

"Change. Do whatever else you need to do to get ready. We'll leave when you're finished."

E scurried to the bathroom to change and slap on a little makeup. Try to calm the racing of her heart, given all that'd happened in the last hour. A literal god sat in the living room. Promised her a worry-free life. A golden existence. But she suspected there was tarnish somewhere in all this, and she couldn't trust herself, or the life he promised. Not completely.

Chapter 4

She'd yelled out the name of the club again through the bathroom door when Plutus, the fucking god, asked her for it. She ignored the sounds of him moving about and talking with no one she could hear, as she got ready. The dress was perfection. It fit her like molten metal poured over skin, clinging to the curves of her breasts and hips and falling so it hid the small but persistent layer of pudge around her midriff. The material shimmered, making her skin glow, the slight pinkish hue shining against the pink in her hair.

E loved makeup, but owned little of it. Only the basics in pharmacy brands, but she'd learned to put it on masterfully over the years. Swiping, brushing, and buffing, she applied a delicate layer of foundation, concealer, blush, highlighter, mascara, and brow gel. An angle brush fluttered over her eye, dusting a thin line of golden shadow there. Last but not least, she added a gloss with a hint of pink the color of her hair to bring it all together. She didn't have the accessories to meet the level of the dress, but looking over herself in the mirror, she thought she looked damn good.

Nerves wiggled down her arms, making her shake out her hands before she turned the doorknob to exit out of the bathroom, out of the apartment, into the night with some god to a glitzy nightclub. Her mouth was half open, ready to call out, when she came face to face with him, leaning against the wall opposite the bathroom. E snapped it closed to stifle the soft scream she almost let loose. A devilish grin lit Plutus's face before a dark light shaded his brilliant green eyes as they moved from her mouth, over her face, down, down, down her body.

His look touched every visible inch of her, and since he was being so damn blatant about it, she did the same. Big mistake. Her eyes flitted over his monochromatic clothing, all black from his suit to his shirt to his tie to his high shine shoes. The only hints of color, in fact, were a gold and diamond tie clip and cufflinks at his wrists before he adjusted his jacket sleeves. When her attention went to those hands, she noticed it for the first time: no claws. When she double-checked, his horns were gone as well. All that remained on his head was his black hair, lush and shining and begging for her to run her hands through it.

"What happened to you?" Rude, she knew, but with so much newness coming at her she didn't have it in her to be polite at the moment.

He waved at the empty space where his tall, spiraling gold horns should be and she nodded. "A charm. Can't go out in all my godly glory, now can I?"

More questions bubbled, but he looked down at what appeared to be a very expensive watch on his left wrist and asked his own. "Are you ready?"

She didn't know how to honestly answer that one in general, but if he meant to go out right that second, she shrugged and she surveyed herself mentally: hair and makeup were all good. She needed to grab her wristlet and transfer things over because she wasn't taking her big ass shoulder bag in this dress. And shoes. Damnit, she'd forgotten all about shoes for the nightclub and this dress to be specific.

The issue turned into a non-issue quickly enough. As if by magic, a pair of shiny pink shoes dangled from one of Pluto's hands when she knew for a fact he'd held nothing a moment before. Of course it was magic, not just like magic. Because he was a damn god. The shoes swung up, and her face came up with them to meet his gaze. Softly, like a caress across her skin, he said, "For you," extending the shoes to her.

They were mules, not too high, and the same color as her hair. Exquisite crystals studded the crisscrossed straps at the toes and she took a moment to be thankful she'd taken the time to give herself a mani-pedi the other night while she watched a rom-com on Netflix. Then she noticed the soles. Blood red.

"Where'd you get these?" Dubious, E eyed them, not taking the shoes from him. The dress was one thing. She figured it was expensive, but she'd checked the label and had no idea who the designer was. Likely meant it was far too rich for her to know, but it gave a certain level of detached deniability. These, however, were distinctive. And distinctly expensive.

An exasperated sigh left the god as he knelt before her. Frozen at the move, at the images it conjured in her heated mind, she stood there like a statue as he raised her left foot first, slipping one of the shoes snugly in place. As he did the same to the other, he looked up, his eyes hitting hers. "I told you, E. Nothing of wealth is hidden from me."

"Meaning you can produce any luxury item out of thin air?" She said this as she shifted her weight back and forth, foot to foot, marveling at the feel of the shoes on her feet. Lisa had a pair of classic black LV heels, had even offered to let E borrow them on occasion, but she'd never dared. She was afraid she'd mess them up, and she didn't have the money to replace something like that. She also feared she'd step into them then miss them when she had to take them off, give them back.

"Yes," he said, all blasé, like being able to produce thousand-dollar shoes at will was no big deal. It made her hackles rise.

"I didn't ask you for any of this."

"Oh, but you did. When you asked to be comfortable. These are as comfortable as women's dress shoes get while still being stylish, I'm afraid."

Once again, too quick for her eye to catch, he moved into her. When he gripped her neck, it was loose, dominant and assertive but not painful or intimidating. Comforting. She found a man's strong, controlling hands on her grounding, depending on the man of course, and Plutus plucked that kinky string in her perfectly. His head cocked to the left and right, the movement of a predator studying.

She felt a weight hit her neck, added to his hand, and one of his now human-looking fingers glided over something at the back of her neck, clicking a clasp into place. She looked down to see a rose gold and diamond necklace resting where his hand had just been.

E closed her eyes, fighting off the dizziness she felt at the absurdity of the entire situation. None of it was believable. For a second she wondered if she'd fallen asleep and dreamed all this. If she did, she could just accept it. Take it all without question. Because it wasn't real.

Plutus leaned in, the whiskey notes of his scent intoxicating, and said, "Come, E. Let's try out this brave new world."

Eyes still closed, she whispered, "With such people in it," and maybe felt a little too much like naive Miranda, given she agreed to follow.

She blinked her eyes opened and really stared for a long minute, searching the fine-tuned bullshit meter she'd gained as a kid in the trailer park. He set off no blaring alarm bells beyond the general warning to not get too close to anyone. She felt at ease with the god, even if she just discovered gods existed. Though, obviously, all of it–the new knowledge of supernaturals, her calling one to her, the way his body made hers sizzle–disoriented her. To steady herself, she fell back on what she knew best: research and learning. "Only if you answer a few of my questions."

A smirk met her demand. "Question for question, then. But first, we leave."

"I need to grab a bag."

"No need."

"Uh, yeah. I have to have my ID, my debit card, my metro card, just in case, and the little bit of cash I have." She'd ticked each thing off on an upraised hand in Pluto's face.

"You only need your ID, and I will carry it for you."

"But..." Damn, she felt like a petulant teenager, ready to stomp a foot, slam the bathroom door in his face, and pout in there for at least an hour. She'd never even done that *as* a teenager because you couldn't slam trailer doors reliably. Probably wouldn't help her now, either. She doubted Plutus was the type to put up with a snit. There'd be no begging or coddling from him, of that she was certain.

"No. You need nothing else when you are with me, and I have multiple pockets." He turned her, his hands scalding on the bare skin of her back, and gently pushed her down the hall. "ID, then we leave and you get your questions."

All of this was insane, but her body moved her forward, tingling under his touch, and she told herself she could go along for a time, to get answers and hopefully a more comfortable life in the future. She'd done the spell, after all. She'd just gotten far more than she bargained for in the process.

Of course there was a dark, expensive car with a huge hood ornament and an attentive driver waiting for them outside her front stoop.

The god's hand smoothed down E's back, causing a shiver in its wake, as he guided her into the back seat. She had to maneuver around a middle console, but she managed without hurting herself or the car. The inside, all plush leather and wood grain accents and clean lines, distracted her until they started gliding down the street.

"So…" She didn't finish, and Plutus looked at her with a sly smile.

"Come on, E. You were the one with questions."

At that, a soft buzzing sounded and a screen came up between them and the driver in front.

"I thought only limos could do that?" Granted, she didn't know much about luxury of any type, but maybe especially luxury cars. Lisa and her parents were the richest people she personally knew, and they were New Yorkers, which meant her friend didn't own a car and usually just used an app, cab, or a discreet car service.

"Is this one of your questions?"

She shook her head no and let it drop. However, she didn't drop the semantics game he'd started. "I need a point of clarification for this little question-and-answer session before we begin."

He inclined his dark head, letting her proceed. "Seems we may need to set some ground rules. I don't think any question I ask you at any given point in time should count."

"Fair enough. How about this? We determine a set number of questions we get, total, and we create an indication for when the questioning begins or ends."

"Twenty questions." E figured everyone, even gods, knew that game.

"Agreed. But twenty questions total. Ten for you and ten for me."

She nodded, brain whirling to come up with the best possible questions she could think of in the moment. His deep, silky voice whispered, "Let's get started."

"Yes, but give me a minute."

He shrugged those massive shoulders and she thought of how wide and tall he was, even in this human form. Which brought her to her first question. "Why and how do gods hide?"

He tsked her way but a spark of amusement lit his brilliant green eyes. "Tricksy E, using compound questions. We did not specify, so I'll allow it."

Plutus leaned back into the black leather seat and turned his head her way. It seemed intimate, like he lay in a bed and looked over at her. She brushed off the idea, and the sexy as hell images it conjured, as he began to talk.

"I assume you know the history of what happened to the supernaturals when they decided to expose themselves to human society."

E sure did. Bloodshed, hunts, general chaos and mayhem, all at the hands of humans. Humans didn't like things that were not like them, and they'd proven it time and time again – with supernaturals and other humans alike.

"But that was centuries ago."

"E, E, E. You know such impulses do not easily die. However, to answer your question of why, first: humans hunted us long before they hunted other supernaturals."

She stared at him, wanting more. Needing more. But she wasn't about to give up a question to get it.

He grinned, as if he knew how she struggled not to ask, and gave it to her anyway. "There is a reason so many stories exist about ancient gods from so many cultures. Because we exist, and at one time, we existed out in the open. Then the humans discovered we were not as invincible as we appeared. What followed was many battles, lots of blood, and many lives lost on both sides."

He sighed deep, his mouth turning down in a frown as if he'd been thrown back into a bad memory. Something in her wanted to soothe those lines on his achingly beautiful face, and she caught her hand as it raised to do just that, clasping it tight in her other and setting it firmly in her lap. Plutus noticed and stared at her lap for several beats before he continued.

"We convened, as we gods so like to do, and came to a decision: we would hide. It took a great deal of magic to make humans think we were myth, but after they thought it, the idea easily passed down from generation to generation. We went about our business, hiding away, or in plain sight, from then on."

A long, silent minute stretched and he chuckled. "You play the game well, E. Let me answer your how question." He began to undo his black silk tie, and E became fascinated by the shape of his hands and the pop of his veins, as he pulled the knot down and unbuttoned the first few buttons on his crisp shirt. A hint of bronze skin gleamed beneath, though it did not have the golden sheen it had earlier.

He snaked two of his long, deft fingers into his shirt and pulled out a necklace. It wasn't shiny and expensive looking, like his tie clip and cufflinks. A skinny brown leather cord, slightly frayed and worn with age, held a dangling bronze medallion. There were markings on it, but in the faint light of the backseat, E couldn't see it clearly.

Curiosity took over and she leaned forward, grabbing the medallion and pulling it, and him, closer to her face. "It looks to be Greek."

"That it is," he purred, so close his breath fanned across her face, smacking her with his delicious smoke and whiskey scent so hard she slammed her eyes closed in defense.

"Sorry," she muttered, dropping the necklace and shoving herself as far back in her seat as she could go.

Plutus stayed where he was, leaning into her space. "You never need to apologize for your impulses with me, E." She was certain he meant more than just her impulse to learn or know, but she kept her mouth zipped.

He slowly eased back into his own seat but kept himself turned toward her, his long legs hitting her own when they stopped and started in the NYC traffic. "My turn."

Plutus made a big show of thinking, tapping his strong chin and tilting his head this way and that. Then, he asked, "Why did you dye your hair pink?"

She blinked at him. Not a hard-hitting question, which surprised her. From what she'd experienced so far, he seemed the calculating sort. E also had to tamp down the urge to ask if he liked it or not. She wasn't going to waste a question on something unnecessary, even if it wormed through her gut.

"Well, my hair is blonde. A dirty blonde, but blonde. I have no problem with it per se, but in college I started dying it various colors. I liked pink the most, so I kept it up."

He stared unblinking, and she knew he wanted more specifics, just like she had. She also knew he wouldn't ask, not during their little game of twenty questions. She decided to give him more. He'd given her blood and terror. E could give him this little bit of herself.

She pulled one side of her hair back and around to expose the left side of her neck. The scars were faint but visible, running from beneath her left ear down to the top of her shoulder. They were far back enough she hid them easily from most people, but she didn't hide them from Plutus. "When I was fourteen, I was trying to make popcorn in a pot because our microwave was broken. There was an accident, hot popcorn kernels and grease flying everywhere. I turned my face in time, thank god, but I was left with this. I eventually got tired of all the questions, even after I healed, and long hair covers them effectively." She gestured to the old scars she was used to after so long, then flipped her hair back in place. "So, I don't like to cut my hair above my shoulders. Which means dyeing it is the only option I have to do something different with it."

Pluto's hand whipped out, curling around the left side of her neck. As he pulled her close, he tilted her head to the side with his surprisingly strong, firm thumb. She let him, and shuddered out a breath when he began to trace the outline of her scars. Then, his face moved in, and his nose butted against her neck. She felt the touch all the way down in her core and she gasped out at the riot in her body.

Half a second later, Plutus was back in his own seat, his nostrils flaring and his eyes glowing green. Not just the brilliant green they were, but literally glowing with a green light. "You have no reason to hide," he ground out. "We all have scars, some more visible than others."

E shrugged and thanked whatever other gods might be around when the car suddenly came to a stop and she heard the driver's side door open and close. "Game over," she whispered as Plutus's door opened from the outside.

His white, human teeth flashed. "Not yet."

She watched him exit and immediately turn to take her hand. It was a horrible idea on so many levels, but her body inched forward and she took what he offered, however much that might be.

Chapter 5

Muggy air hit E in the face. No matter the number of summers she lived there, she didn't think she'd ever get used to it. At least in Columbus, or even Middletown, she'd been able to find space in the heat. Here, however, the humidity mixed with the hard concrete and brick and the mass of people, making her sometimes feel like she was swimming, jostling with others to get air when she needed it.

Plutus pulled her tight to his side. A little too tight, she noticed, when his hand dug a touch too hard into her hip. A sound rumbled into the air and it took her a moment to realize it came from deep in Plutus's chest. A growl? Surely not—but when she placed her hand on his chest, she felt the vibration.

E looked up to his face, worry etching her own, and turned her head slowly to see where his stony green eyes stared. Ahead of them, leaning against the brick wall beside the recessed door of the club, a thin, pale man stared back, fangs slightly bared. He may have also growled, for all E knew, but they were too far away. Apparently this club had a vampire bouncer, which was damn smart. They were faster and stronger than humans and had heightened senses. All good things for security detail. However, it didn't seem great in terms of how Plutus reacted.

He clipped out, "Stay close to me, E."

E rolled her eyes but followed his lead. Vamps weren't super common in her circles, but she'd run into enough of them to in her few years in NYC to not be fazed. They were often safer to be around than humans, who seemed to always cause the most trouble wherever they were. Still, it looked like the vampire and Plutus might have some aggressive standoff or something, so she kept her opinions to herself. She didn't want to think about what a fight between a vampire and a god might entail.

The vampire peeled his lanky frame off the brick, looking to most in the crowd like he stepped easy, but E saw the slight crinkle around his eyes, his rapid look between her and Plutus, the flare of his nostrils. He practically screamed unease, to her.

To Plutus as well, whose growl turned up a notch as he stepped closer. Thankfully, he stopped a few feet away. "I haven't seen you in a while."

Plutus simply nodded, a clipped, hard gesture.

"Yours?" the vampire asked, gesturing toward me with the flip of a hand.

Another clipped nod from Plutus.

"There will be no trouble in here because you decided to take her out for the night?" It could be construed as a demand, but the lilt made it a question. A vampire asking a god if they will behave.

"I will keep her close. You have my word."

This time, the vampire gave a clipped nod before he turned to the side, gesturing them forward with a sweep of his hand. No line for them, then.

Plutus tugged her along, and she matched his big strides for a few steps before he slowed, forcing his legs to move in more measured steps so they matched their pace. Once inside the big brick building, the music engulfed them, forcing out all her thoughts as she adjusted.

Before she could say or do anything, a dark-haired woman in a short, black, bandage dress wielding a small tablet steeped toward Plutus. "This way, sir." She gestured for them to follow her to the left of the hallway, which was the opposite direction from where a wide hole in the hallway poured out music and flickered with light.

They moved to a small hall hidden behind a thick black curtain, one E finally realized wound behind and then above the side of the club, bringing them up a small set of stairs until they went through yet another black curtain. She blinked at the pulses of light and the wash of a deep purple glow illuminating everything. Hell. They were in the elevated VIP area on the outskirts of the massive dance floor. She'd glimpsed this part of the club the one time she'd been here with Lisa and her crowd. They hadn't even had enough pull to get a table up there, though they had snagged one of the booths lining the dance floor, which was a win in and of itself, from the excitement she'd seen from Lisa when they'd gotten it.

She said nothing, sticking tight to Plutus's side, as she said she would, until the woman stopped and gestured toward a circular booth along the wall. "Kim will be with you shortly," she added with a small nod of her head before moving away to handle whatever business she had to handle.

The music felt slightly muted here, though it still poured hard over her, thumping through her body. Plutus gave her a small nudge forward so she scooted into the booth first, stopping halfway around when he snaked an arm around her shoulders to hold her still so he could come in close to her. From this position, they could see part of the dance floor, the DJ booth, and also hear one another if they leaned into each other's ears.

The woman came over with a tablet perched on a serving tray. "Welcome. I'm Kim. I'll be your server for the evening. She pointed at a small divot in the middle of the table where E noticed a tiny silver button. "At any time, press this, and I'll be here in a flash." She also flashed a smile at them before asking what they wanted. "Vodka soda. Double." E'd learned a while ago ordering a vodka soda was simple enough and usually a solid choice wherever she was. She had anxiety about looking foolish in new places, like someone might figure out she didn't belong. A vodka soda meant she didn't have to think, or overthink, a drink choice.

"Top shelf." Plutus cocked his head in thought, then said, "Chopin." A small smile lit on the waitress's face as she went through menus on her tablet to mark the order. "I will have a Macallan 30." He reached into the inside pocket of his suit jacket before the waitress finished, plucking a shiny black credit card to hand to the woman. She tapped it on her screen, paused a moment, then handed it back before chirping "I'll be right back with those drinks," and leaving them alone.

So much had happened in the last ten minutes, she'd forgotten the heat of him until the sear on her side reminded her. Thinking snark might help her out a bit, she leaned into him more and asked, "No magicking the drinks like you did with the shoes and dress? And suit?" None of that'd been in her apartment, so he'd had to get it some supernatural way.

He chuckled, reached a hand over to stroke her cheek before he turned her head away and dipped low. His mouth was warm and so damn close to her ear it didn't take much to imagine what it'd feel like latched there. "No need. I have the means to pay. Because of my particular skills, I do rather well in the stock market."

Figured he was a Wall Street type. He almost fit the finance bro mold. If it wasn't for those little moments of sweetness she'd seen glimmering through.

She pushed the idea of his potential sweetness down deep. E didn't need to think on it. They had a transactional relationship, nothing more. She didn't want more, not from anyone. She needed to get herself straight however she could then keep herself that way. It was all she could trust in after years of being in survival mode: herself.

Instead of focusing on who he may or may not be, she went in a different direction.

"The scene out front was a little wild." Plutus didn't seem to need her to be right in his ear to hear what she said, but he stayed buried in her pink hair so she could hear him.

"Apologies, E. It was... surprising to see the vampire there. I may have overreacted. He was right to check I wouldn't act the same way inside."

"There are vampires around the city, Plutus. You should get used to them."

A soft chuckle puffed across her ear and she shivered. "I am used to vampires, E. I am, however, unused to vampires being in your vicinity."

Whatever the hell that meant. E considered, thinking about how she and a vampire might have an issue, but she came up with nothing. It felt territorial, which might be because of who she was to Plutus. Whatever a human was to a god when they struck a deal. She imagined the inverse, the idea of him in the same space as someone she might consider dangerous. For a second, a word flashed hard and insistent in her mind: *MINE*. Shock and confusion echoed after it, even if the word rang true to her.

Lucky for her, Kim popped back up with their drinks, so she could shove the thoughts away with booze. E scooped up her glass, push aside the straw, and sucked down a good bit of the pint-sized vodka soda the waitress deposited in front of her. She had to admit, whatever the fancy-ass vodka was, it went down a lot smoother than the liquor she usually got when on any of her rare nights out.

"Easy there, E," Plutus shouted at her. He'd moved his head away from hers to grab his scotch and thank the waitress. Courteous and kind to service workers was another fact she wasn't going to know about Plutus. She instead narrowed her eyes on him and concentrated on his words.

"You have no say in how easy I do or don't go."

A smirk lifted his lips and she thought she'd like to see his fangs there instead of the flash of regular old human teeth. "Do you not like it easy, E?"

She wasn't going to touch that question. Nope. Instead, she took another deep pull of her drink and turned her attention to the dance floor below them. E swayed to the EDM music pumping through the air, letting her mind drift to sound rather than the insanity of her night and the waves of heat coming from the man beside her.

"Would you like to dance?" he asked.

E nodded, thinking she might get away from him on the dance floor, and took another huge swallow of her drink, making ice clink her glass. Jesus, had she actually drunk almost that whole thing in three big chugs? She hadn't done something like that since she was a college freshman.

She let the glass drift down to the table before she shook away the maudlin thoughts starting to creep in. At the shake, the fact she'd been tipsy once already that night crashed into her. She'd sobered when Plutus appeared in her apartment, but the wine drunk was now mixing with a too-quick vodka buzz. It likely meant bad things for her. But, god, she needed it after all that'd happened that day and night.

Plutus scooted out of the opposite side of the booth, bending deep to offer his hand. She took it without hesitation, although she'd known him for less than three hours at this point. Didn't matter, in her hazy mind. Her gut, which she trusted, said he wouldn't hurt her. Physically, at least. She couldn't trust he'd keep her intact in other important ways, even if her gut also told her he just might be a good dude.

She couldn't trust others with her emotions, with her future, but she could trust them physically. Sexually even, which her drunk mind automatically went to when his large, veiny hand gripped hers and he tugged her forward with just the right amount of force. Her thoughts made her body clench and Plutus's eyes widened as his nostrils flared. Oh, hell. He'd somehow sensed how her body reacted to him.

Did it matter he knew? She wanted him, and she could have him. In this way. She was no prude. She'd had a string of sexual partners, some she even dated briefly. Her latest dry spell had lasted eight months, and Plutus could help her end it.

"Come." He gripped her waist when she tottered slightly as she stood, before leading her to a different set of stairs leading down into a roped-off section of the dance floor, one less populated but still filled with moving bodies. The word on his lips made her want to pant, and she was thankful there was so much sensory input in this place he might miss it if she did. Unlikely, as he seemed constantly trained on her, but he might.

Once they hit a dark corner of the VIP dance section, he spun around, pulling her close to his body by her waist. They fit well despite the height difference. She still had to crane her neck far back to look up in his face as she started to move to the music.

Her arms went up on their own accord, wrapping around his neck so her hands hung limp from her wrists behind his head. One of his hands shot up, tracing an invisible line from the underside of her forearm, past her elbow, over her shoulder, and down the back side of the thin strap of her glittering dress. Her body bucked at the feel of his light touch, causing her hips to push against his.

She thought she heard a hiss slither out of his mouth, but all her attention stayed on the way their hips ground against each other to the thump, thump, thump of the music in perfect time to make her melt if there weren't all these pesky clothes between them. She ground down harder and pushed her chest closer to his, brushing her hardening nipples against the lush fabric of her dress and his suit, sending a zip of awareness down her spine.

'Damnit, E." Plutus turned them and walked her back until she hit wall. A darkened wall, where Plutus's body covered her own. He dipped his head down and ran his nose from the tip of her chin up her jaw before he nestled his mouth right at her ear once again. "You glow in this light. Look good enough to eat right here and now."

She managed to say, "Yes, please." Or so she thought. It came out garbled.

Plutus pulled back slightly and bit out a curse that didn't sound fun. "Look at me, E."

It took her a moment, and she couldn't focus completely.

He said, "We're leaving," tugging on her hand.

She dug her lovely new shoes in and stopped him, but only because he apparently didn't want to drag her out of the club when he very clearly could. "I want to dance with you, Plutus." She trailed a finger up from his shining belt buckle to the knot of his tie, pulling on it until he leaned hard into her.

"We will dance more, E. I swear it. Just not tonight. It's time to go home."

At the idea of home, which meant bed, and maybe meant Plutus in the bed, she nodded. A touch too vigorously, because it made her sway on her feet. At that, Plutus curved one strong arm around her waist, helping her stay steady. He texted something on his phone as they moved slowly up the stairs. He stopped Kim on the way and thanked her, signing her tablet before they moved back down the secret, rich-person passage, and out of the club. He even nodded at the vampire who now looked more amused than anything else.

The car idled at the curb once again and she didn't need to be told to climb into it. Plutus cussed again, moving quickly to cover what might have been a crotch shot for anyone in the crowd if he wasn't so damn fast. "Home," he ground out as the driver closed the door on them.

"Home," E repeated as she snuggled into the soft leather of the seat. "Turn the AC up, will you?"

Plutus sighed but did as she asked. The cool air caused goosebumps to jump all over but she only snuggled deeper into the seat.

"I should have been more conscious of what you've had to drink," Plutus muttered as if he talked to himself. As if he admonished himself for not taking proper care of her.

"How were you supposed to know I drank almost a whole bottle of wine before you even showed at my place?"

A sliver of menace traced his words when he said, "If these were different circumstances, you'd receive swift punishment when we got back to your apartment."

"What, you going to spank me, daddy?"

"Yes." The single word was solid. Definitive. Held no quarter.

"Delicious," E whispered, but the cool air, soft leather seat, alcohol, and Plutus's deep voice all dragged her down into drowsiness. "Talk to me," she commanded.

"What do you want me to say?"

"Anything. I just like your voice."

There was a long pause, then Plutus started reading off signs he saw out the window. Ray's Dry Cleaning. Fix-A-Phone. First Light Bagels and Coffee. The names blurred together as E's lids grew heavier and heavier, and Plutus's voice followed her into sleep, where she might have even heard it in her dreams.

If she could remember them.

Chapter 6

E struggled back to reality. She'd had a lot to drink the night before, and she'd mixed alcohols. Even in her mid-twenties, that was a bad idea. Hence the dull headache and the Sahara-level dry mouth as she rapidly blinked her gummy eyes open. *Ugh*.

She also doubted she'd washed her face when she'd gotten home, as she didn't remember even getting home, and caked mascara was likely not helping the whole situation.

The discomfort eased with a solid minute of laying prone, but it didn't last long. Memories of last night, and Plutus, flashed in her mind and she sat straight up in bed, a little frantic. She thought it might have been a dream. But when she threw the covers off her bed, she saw proof it was all too real: her glittery, expensive rose gold dress still clung to her body. E groaned deep, smacking her slightly pounding head in her hands.

Her curtain door flung back, and there stood the huge, disarmingly sexy, god in the flesh. In his beastly, gold-dusted flesh instead of human flesh, which somehow made him even hotter to her. He held out a tall glass of water in one hand and two ibuprofens in his other. "Take these."

"Bossy," she muttered, shooting him a glare, but she grabbed the water and let him dump the pills in her upturned palm. He was right, though she wouldn't say as much out loud. The water cooled her as she took more than a few big gulps. Those gulps brought back memories of her slamming the vodka soda. Then being all over Plutus. She wasn't exactly embarrassed by it. Hell, he looked good enough to eat eyeing her right then, even with the pounding headache. She would, however, calm such urges for now until she had a better understanding of what was to come with him.

"What now?"

A flash of teeth. "Are we playing 20 questions again?"

E shook her head no. "I'll call it that when we are. We can't just go around making every question we ask during the day count. There needs to be a designated time and space for that, especially since I only get nine more questions."

Plutus nodded in agreement. "We start the game only when we both agree to do so."

Good enough for her, so she didn't respond. She did try to slide around his body and found herself a little wobbly on her feet, which caused her to tilt forward a little too far. Right into the god's bare-ish chest. He was wearing his silky, pristine toga again, but it left a whole lot of chest real estate open for her hands to explore.

E sensed the odd tingle and tug she'd felt last night, heightened by his warm skin under her hands. He shifted and she looked up to see his bright green eyes blown out wide, like a big cat with prey in its sights. It took some real willpower, but she managed to peel her hands off his flesh and turned on her heels to give herself a little space from his hungry look.

"Could you…" she gestured behind her with a flailing hand. "I need to change."

He said nothing, but the sound of her curtain being tugged back across the plastic tension rod above her head, and the cold space where he'd once stood was enough of an answer. She reached over to her sad little dresser and pulled out a pair of old sweatpants and a too-large t-shirt advertising the donut shop where she worked as an undergrad. Comfy, and not at all sexy. It might help, but she doubted it.

After she snagged a claw clip from the top of her dresser and secured her mass of pink hair in a twist at the back of her head, she shuffled out. She expected to see the mess she'd left in the living room the night before, but everything appeared to be back to normal. Except the sofa and coffee table were a little off from where they had been, leaving more space between her room and the living room area. The same space she'd used to call up Plutus from the faint grit of chalk dust she saw there.

"Thank you," she said, nodding to the area. She sure as hell hadn't cleaned up last night, so Plutus had done it, with his hands or his magic.

He sat, legs wide and arms stretched along the back of the sofa, and nodded his acknowledgement, his metallic, curved horns glinting in the morning light as they dipped down. Two coffee cups sat on the table in front of him, along with two waxy paper bags. She breathed deep, wanting the little coffee scent pick-me-up, but what rushed into her was the smell of tarnished metal, smoke, and whiskey. The distinct scent she now knew was all Plutus.

He leaned down to snag a cup of coffee and bring it to those luscious, full lips. "Help yourself," he muttered before taking a drink.

She held up a finger in the universal "give me a minute" gesture and shuffled to the bathroom, where she took care of business, ran a cold washrag over her face to get some sort of clean, and quickly brushed her teeth. Before going back to the living room, she made a detour to the kitchen to fill one of her water bottles with the Brita filter in the fridge.

"Do you not drink coffee?" Plutus gestured toward her water bottle before she sat beside him and took a deep drink.

She pushed herself over, letting her back hit the edge of the couch and her legs curl up underneath her so she faced the god lounging in her apartment. "Yep. Just need to hydrate a little first." E leaned over, moved the untouched coffee closer, then snatched up one of the waxy paper bags. She took a peek and sighed in happiness. Inside she found a buttery croissant, split open and stuffed with melted cheese and bacon. Fatty goodness to help the water and meds wrestle the mild hangover hovering over her.

She hummed to herself as she took several bites of the sandwich, a habit she had whenever she enjoyed food. E usually tried to control it around people she didn't know well, much like the little odd noises she made when working or studying. She didn't seem to mind doing it around Plutus.

Mid-bite she looked up to find his eyes trained on her, his lips quirked up so his large fangs were on full display. "Sorry," she managed to say after swallowing.

"No need to apologize, little one."

"Why 'little one'?"

He waved a hand at himself, then at her, and repeated: "Little. One."

Whatever. As far as nicknames went, it wasn't too bad, so she let it slide. She'd been called much worse by men before.

Plutus scooped up his own sandwich and began eating it, settling into a somehow comfortable silence. Eventually, he wiped his hands with a napkin and asked, "Do you have plans for today?"

E had a second to think about it because she'd just taken a drink of her coffee. She took a moment to savor the rich, bold flavor of it and hummed again before she answered. "I normally work on thesis things or run personal errands on Saturdays. I don't have to go to my internship on weekends, so it's a good time for me to catch up on regular life things or writing and research."

"If I were not here, which would you do?"

"Likely both. Run errands then do research into the night. Maybe veg out with some romcom or historical drama. That's my usual Saturday."

His hand, outstretched on the couch still, skimmed across her own for a brief heartbeat and it sent a thrill down her spine. "I'd like to take you out again in a calmer environment. Do you have time today?"

She went over her mental to-do list. She could realistically put off research for one day. However, she did need to go by the pharmacy and grocery store if she didn't want to skip her birth control and eat for the next week. "I need to hit up a few places, but I don't need to research today if I can focus on it tomorrow."

"Good," he practically purred in his deep voice and flicked his had in the air in an odd way. "We'll run your errands then have a day out."

"I'm taking a shower first," she said, rising from the couch as she crumpled her dirty sandwich paper in her hand.

His forked, intriguingly tensile, tongue flicked out, tracing his upper lip and fangs, and her knees nearly buckled. Instead of waiting around to see what he might say with that sly glint in his eyes, she scurried toward her room to gather clothes.

The day was nearly derailed a minute later when she threw back her room curtain to find her closet stuffed to the brim with new, expensive looking clothes. Not like regular expensive either. Like old-money classic lines and fancy fabrics. So old money she only recognized half the designer tags she saw. She went out to argue with Plutus about it, but he simply said, "You asked to be comfortable. The clothes are part of our deal."

They were soft and cool and would be perfectly comfortable, goddammit, and though she stomped back to the bathroom, she didn't argue. She picked out one of the linen button-up shirts he'd somehow put in her room while they had breakfast. She paired that with an old, worn-in pair of Levi's she'd picked up at a thrift store and her trusty sandals with the appropriate amount of style and cushion for a woman who walked around the city more often than not.

She muttered more expletives when a leather crossbody purse lay bold as you please on her bed when she returned after her shower/makeup/dressing routine. Soft as butter and smelling strongly of Plutus, she eyed it suspiciously before going for her own plain-Jane, serviceable purse, which already had her sunglasses in it. She transferred her wallet and headphones in it before scrambling to find her phone. Until she remembered Plutus had it, along with her ID.

"I need my things from last night," she huffed out, hip cocked and sharp eyes right on him. He'd changed out of his toga and into his own worn jeans and a black t-shirt that fit a touch too snuggly over those big arms and that delicious chest of his. She pushed those thoughts deep down where she locked away all the other lustful imaginings she'd had in the brief time she'd known this guy and waited for his response. He stared down at his own phone and said, "They're on the kitchen table."

E stopped cold three steps there, which was honestly about halfway given the size of the open space in the apartment. Her ID sat on top of a shiny new phone and laptop, nicer than anything she'd ever owned. Hell, her current smartphone worked well, but it still had a headphone jack on it. She kind of liked it, though, because it made her listening and tuning others out far more obvious than most wireless buds.

"No. No. Nu-uh."

"Problem?" He cooed from the couch, now giving her his full attention.

"Yes. Big problem. This isn't going to work."

"The phone and laptop? They should be compatible with anything you have."

"Not like that, and don't be obtuse. I mean this whole thing isn't going to work. Not if you just go about replacing all my things willy-nilly."

"But yours were old and not as good as you could have."

"They were what I have. What I'm used to, which is important when I have things to do." She stomped over and snatched up the laptop, holding it out like it was a snake that'd bite her. "Does this thing even have my files on it?" Then the real horror hit her and she sagged. "Where's my old laptop?"

When Plutus didn't answer fast enough, she yelled the question, "Where is it!?!"

"Calm down-" he started but she cut him off with a look that could melt glass and a voice dripping with condemnation. "Pro tip, your godliness: modern women don't like to be told to 'calm down.' Particularly when they have a very fucking valid reason to not be calm. Like when a god throws out a laptop that holds all the work you've done for the last two years."

"Do you not use the cloud?"

"Yes, but I need backups on backups, buddy. I need that laptop. Now."

He held his hands up in a placating gesture she might call condescending if his face wasn't the picture of contrition. "Apologies, E. I didn't realize."

"Of course you didn't. Because you assumed what you wanted was best. But I'm sure you know what happens when you assume, hmm?"

He chuckled, and she didn't see anything funny about the situation, but the soft sound made her stomach do an odd flip despite the anger still flowing fast in her veins.

With a flick of his wrist, her laptop appeared on top of the new machine, along with her old smartphone. He stepped closer, too close, his heat burning into her like their clothes weren't even there. Anger lingered still, but so did the idea he was hers and she was his, absurd as it was. She barely knew the guy.

"E, I am truly sorry. From now on, we will discuss me replacing any of your things."

"And you giving me things." She wanted to push, partially so she could stop feeling so damn weird about him giving her things but so she could push him, see how far she could go with the god.

Another deep chuckle and she was well aware he didn't confirm or deny her last point. His hand jumped out in a flash, twisting a pink lock of hair around one perfectly sharp, golden claw. He stared at it, rubbing it between two fingers, before looking at her pink-glossed lips and stepping away. "Come," he commanded. "We have places to go."

They went to the pharmacy and the small grocery store next to it, picking up essentials for the week ahead. They had two mini-fights at the cash registers, with E winning at the pharmacy because she started talking about bodily autonomy and the cashier, who E exchanged pleasantries with weekly, gave him the stink eye until he relented. Plutus won at the grocery store because he'd thrown in extra things at the last minute and claimed he'd be eating at her apartment for the foreseeable future, so he should be allowed to chip in on food.

The same car and driver had taken them to and fro, and waited as she and Plutus carried the bags up to her apartment and put the cold things in her fridge as quickly as possible.

Once the car door shut them into their nice leather cocoon, she asked, "Where to now?"

"MOMA."

She loved the Museum of Modern Art. Because she lived in the Village and it was closer, and because it had awesome views, she'd spent more time at the Whitney, but there was something special about MOMA. She thought museums were a great way to spend a muggy June afternoon, so she didn't question it and didn't even fuss when he didn't ask about tickets, or use her student ID for a discount. Mainly because he'd purchased the tickets on his phone at some point and flashed the barcode to the employee before she could say anything about it.

They started at the top floor and Plutus gave her a little more than he needed to without them playing their question game. "It has been well over two decades since I've been here."

Because he offered up information, she did the same. "I came here six months ago, but I would come once a week if I had the time and money. I love a good museum, whether it's art or history."

Plutus nodded; his now-human hands clasped behind his back in a casual stance. They stopped in front of a Paul Cezanne piece titled Pines and Rocks. The white streaks of light in the murky blue around the pines drew her eye and she risked a different, more personal question, without the confines of twenty questions. "Have you known many artists?"

His head turned to her, cocked, as if assessing. His answer said he was more than willing to go through the opening she created. "Some. Not many go into the arts for wealth and luxury, which is my forte. Sadly, I often see their products years later. I have met a few in my many years, however. Just not as many as other gods who dabble in art directly."

He asked his own question in turn. "What's your favorite piece at this museum?"

A sad smile stretched across her mouth, and she took his hand, leading him down a few flights of stairs and into a small alcove off one of the main hallways. It was the entry to a larger room, and a person could miss the painting here it if they weren't paying attention. There on the right, a few steps from the entryway into the other space, was a small-ish canvas. The frame of simple mid-grain wood highlighted both the painting and its almost lonely space on the wall. Not for the first time, E thought whoever placed it here, like this, was a genius. It helped highlight the isolation and longing in the piece.

"*Christina's World*. Andrew Wyeth." It wasn't the most famous piece at MOMA, but also not the most obscure. Enough people knew about the painting that it got traffic, but not anything like the Picassos or Pollocks in their collection. It was also a deceptively simple painting. It showed an older farmhouse in the distance, with a barn and a few outbuildings around it. A sea of grassy hills stretched between those buildings in the background and the woman lying in a pale pink everyday dress, turned like she was reaching toward the house in the foreground, her dark hair pulled back but with strands floating in the breeze.

"Why is this your favorite?" The question wasn't judgmental but curious. Plutus wanted to know what about the painting called to something in her.

"The painting is beautiful, of course. The colors are muted but gorgeous. The background and foreground have subtle and engaging detail. But it's what you find out about the subject that makes it more impactful." She pointed to the woman. "See, Christina here actually lived on this farm. She was a neighbor to Wyeth for most of his life. She had a muscular disease, likely polio or something given the time period. She wouldn't use a wheelchair, instead, she would crawl where she needed to go. Which limited where she could go, you see."

She turned, faced him fully as he was already staring intently at her. There was something important there she needed him to get. "The title? It's her world. Her whole world. She was confined by her circumstances."

Plutus thought a beat then said, "Bittersweet."

A piece of frost shook free from E's heart at the word. It was perfect for the painting. The image and the history melded care, concern, longing, and need together. All for a woman who may have had more but couldn't because of something she had no control over. A feeling E understood.

Without thinking, propelled to move by the word off his lips, she went up on her tiptoes, planted her hands on his massive shoulders to give her additional leverage, and put her lips on his.

E intended it to be a short, sweet kiss. An acknowledgement they both saw the beautiful thing in front of them. What she intended didn't come to pass, though, because as soon as her lips met his, a chain tugged tight in her gut, wound around his body, and sucked them in close. Or so it felt. She plastered herself to his body, needing to feel as much of him as possible.

Plutus twined his limbs around her, holding her close, leaving no air between them. He pushed forward at the same time, forcing E's head back as he hungrily sucked on her lips before her mouth gasped open. Then her tongue was in play, wrestling with his sinfully nimble one. A tinge of desperation drifted over them, as if they needed more and could never have it. As if they'd waited their whole lives to be right there but now needed something different.

A moan swelled in her chest, passed from her to Plutus, and he swallowed it up. His hands roamed down, gripped tight on her ass, and she almost jumped up on him. Nearly wrapped her legs around his waist so she could grind into his hard body.

Almost and nearly because he pulled away a split second later, a growl low in his throat. Then E heard a muttered, "Sorry, dude," as two snickering guys in their early twenties backed away from the doorway.

"Unbelievable," Plutus hissed out. She felt mortified, so she tried to move away.

Except she was still locked up tight in his arms. "Oh, no, little one. No retreat for you now."

"I'd rather not put on a show for more people," she muttered, trying to tug herself away then.

A deep, long-suffering sigh came from Plutus. "I suppose you are right." He softly caressed her ass one final time then releasing his grip. "Know this is not over. You let me in, E. I won't be locked out again."

E wasn't stupid. She was a grad student at a prestigious university, for god's sake. But she couldn't figure out if he was talking about the conversation or the kiss. The scary thing was, she didn't know if she was more concerned with her letting him into her body or her heart.

Chapter 7

Plutus didn't push his advantage, much to E's relief. She'd been embarrassed in the museum not because she was kissing someone in public, but because she'd nearly lost control from a simple kiss. He'd tasted as good as he smelled, and the smoky notes of his lips lingered long after their kiss. She wanted him, damnit, which might be fine in theory. She'd had one-night stands in the past. Sex with men she didn't know well didn't rattle her. The fact she had to hang around with the god for another month afterward might make it awkward. Oh, and the fact he was a freaking god and he acted like he wanted more than simple sex upped the complication factor.

All of this meant E heaved a big old sigh of relief when Plutus didn't try anything in the more private confines of the car when it picked them up from the museum. He ignored her doing something on his phone. She tried to ignore him also, but it was damn hard when heat seemed to roll off him in waves, seeping into her skin. She craned her neck, trying to see what he was doing.

"All you need to do is ask, E." Without even looking at her, he'd caught her snooping.

"It's fine."

A snort came from the god. "Even I know 'fine' means not fine for most human women."

"Have you been with many human women?" The question popped right from her mouth without thought. E had no idea where it came from, or why a pit formed in her stomach at the thought of what he could say.

Plutus slowly lowered his phone and turned his body in the seat so he could face her more fully. "I'll answer that, little one. *If* we are playing twenty questions."

Well, shit. She wanted the answer, but did she want it enough to waste one of her remaining questions on it? The word *mine* echoed in her mind again, roared actually, and she had to know. "Fine. Twenty questions. Again, have you been with many human women?"

"Define many," he said, a slow smile spread across his full lips. When E huffed at the reply, he laughed, a whip crack sound she felt down to her toes. "I'm not trying to be evasive, E. It is an honest response. I've lived for millennia, so any answer I give could well be many if I am judged by human standards."

She hadn't thought of that. She wanted to ask more; about his apparently long life, how he survived through human history, why he seemed so comfortable in her world when he'd lived through so much history already. E managed to keep her trap shut, because the game was afoot. Instead, she nodded in acknowledgement and really thought about what he said. "Let me revise my question: how many human women have you spent time with like this?"

"None."

"I doubt that." If he wasn't going to honest with her, what was the point of their little question game? She leaned back into her seat, her arms folding around her middle, turning to look out the window and watch the city slide by.

A hot, strong hand gripped her thigh. "E, look at me." The command in his voice made him hard to ignore. Oh, she tried. For all of ten seconds, before he said, "E," again and squeezed her upper thigh. Something in her couldn't not look his way.

"I did not lie. I will not lie. Not to you." His green eyes blazed into her brown ones, dragging her down into their depths. "You asked a specific question, and I answered. I have never spent extended periods of time with a human woman. Until now, I had no reason to do so."

E wanted to press, but she didn't ask all the questions his answer brought up. The biggest one being, why me?

The hand at her thigh rose to her face, cupped her cheek. "You are unique to me, E."

Not special. Unique. Maybe they were similar enough, but there was a distinction in her mind. Special meant valuable. Unique meant one of a kind in general. The single word stung far more than it should, but helped her reinforce the wall she needed to erect around her heart. The wall she'd had no problem keeping in place prior to Plutus.

"I believe you," she said. She did believe him. Whatever brought them together, tied her up in him, helped her believe.

"My turn," he declared, his thumb gently stroking her cheek. A clawless thumb, she thought with more than a little disappointment.

He moved back, leaned against his door to give her some space. "What is your thesis topic?"

Her forehead crinkled in confusion. He didn't make her ask why. He shook his phone in his hand. "After I made reservations for the evening, I did a quick search on your name. Found some of your conference presentations. It made me curious."

"Okay..." If he wanted to waste his questions—which seemed to be a pattern given his first question was about her hair—she'd let him. Plus, her thesis was a safe topic. The city continued to zoom by as she talked at length about her research on the intersection between book preservation and college curriculum. How one can help the other, with the right relationships. As she spoke, Plutus tilted his head toward her whenever he wanted to ask a question. He couldn't outright ask, she knew, because they were technically still in their game. His desire to know, however, came through loud and clear. Which caused a different, maybe more dangerous, tingle to race through her than the one when they kissed in the museum.

And she found herself giving him what he wanted every time.

Chapter 8

E's discussion of her research lasted until they pulled into her apartment. Plutus said there was something he needed to do, so he would leave her for two hours, when they needed to leave for their early dinner reservation at some fancy pants restaurant she didn't know. She sagged in relief at the idea she'd have a few hours by herself to think through things.

And think she did. Maybe obsess better described it. E took a full hour to go over what she didn't know, what she needed to know versus what she wanted to know, and how she could get those answers from the eight questions she had left in their little game. Then she took an hour to get ready, all the while tweaking the questions in her mind as she put on makeup, did her hair, and got dressed.

Her mind also wandered to their kiss. The way she felt whenever he touched her. The need she sensed driving her. She decided she'd slake her lust with Plutus. Dial back the sexual tension by giving into it. Or at least she hoped that'd be the way it'd play out.

When a knock sounded at her door, she startled out of those thoughts and strolled over to open the door. Leading with a little snark, she said, "I figured you'd just come on in."

Her mouth snapped shut when she saw him standing there, perfectly tailored charcoal suit molded to his massive body. His hair looked tousled and his blazing green eyes moved up and down her body. She wore a little black dress Plutus had added to her closet with all the other new clothes earlier that morning and the strappy pink mules he'd given her the night before. She'd been unhappy about him pushing expensive things on her when she hadn't asked for them, didn't need them, but knowing she'd be in a fancy restaurant made her happier he had done it. Given how Plutus looked like crisp money in front of her, she'd made the right decision. The lust in his eyes didn't hurt, either.

"Would you like to come in?" she asked, her voice husky to her own ears.

Plutus tucked his chin in, his eyes hard and heated. "If I do, we'll miss our reservation."

She didn't think that was a bad thing at the moment, but before she could say so, he grabbed her hand and tugged her into his body. The sear of heat made her breath go out in a rush. Her mouth hung open as she craned her neck to look up into his face. A growl came out before he dipped down and kissed her, swift and hard, his lips a promise. E knew with certainty they'd have sex. Very soon. But with each second his lips explored her mouth, she lost confidence in the idea it'd take one night to get him out of her system.

After a too-short minute, he pulled away. "You look devastatingly beautiful, E."

When she caught her breath, she quipped, "You don't look too bad yourself."

He laughed full and deep, which made her heart pound to a different beat. More mellow, less lustful, but no less profound. "Come. We have places to be."

Plutus led her through the restaurant. Because of the name, she'd known it was on Park Avenue, but until they pulled up in the car, she hadn't realized it was in Billionaire's Row, taking up an entire floor in a tall complex. The expense of it made her want to cave in on herself. It was too much. For anyone, but definitely for a girl who was only a few years removed from the trailer park.

When Plutus let go of her hand so she could take a seat at their cozy table with a view of Central Park, E felt unmoored. Nervous. Maybe even vulnerable. Like people could look at her and know she didn't belong. It was a feeling she was familiar with. One she hated but couldn't escape. Or hadn't yet managed to escape.

She tucked a strand of pink hair behind her ear as she took her seat and trained her eyes firmly on the exquisite tablecloth and gleaming table setting. She sensed Plutus seating himself across from her, but she didn't look up at him. He called her name.

Clearing her throat as if it would help steel her nerves, she asked, "Yes?" She still didn't look at him, though. She looked out the window. Took a sip of water the felicitous waiter brought over as soon as they sat.

"Look at me, little one," he huffed out on a low whisper.

She finally looked up into his face to see worry etched there.

"What's wrong? Do you not like the restaurant? We can leave." He half stood before she could stop him.

"No. No. Please, sit. Sit down." She rushed out, hoping no one noticed.

"Okay," he said, easing back down in his chair, though a deep v still stood out between his slash of dark brows. "Tell me what's wrong."

She leaked air like a balloon, before she looked around to see if anyone looked their way. No one did, so she leaned deep across the table and whispered. "I don't belong here."

Plutus smirked. Right in her face. "Of course you do."

The dismissal made her bristle, and she clung to her annoyance. "I'm a pink-haired girl from a trailer park in Ohio. So, no, I most definitely don't belong here."

He studied her before he said, "There is no need to be nervous, E."

Of course there was.

"You see the couple two tables over on our right?"

She quickly looked over to take them in and shifted her eyes back to Plutus. "Yeah."

"The man is up to his eyeballs in SEC trouble. And the woman knows they are drowning in debt but keeps on spending."

"Plutus!" She hissed out, afraid they might've heard him.

However, he kept going. "The table closest to the kitchen is new money made from exploiting labor laws in East Asia, and they're seething they don't have a better table." He threw his head back slightly, indicating a group of men laughing a bit too hard behind him. "They are all hedge fund managers who bought up a mass of single-family house in various areas in the country, driving up prices so they could make more money and fewer people could afford their own homes."

She couldn't help the way her nose crinkled in disgust at all this information.

"However, it's not all bad," he said, sliding his eyes to her right so she saw two old women, heads bent low together. "Those two used the old family money they got from long-dead husbands to help them live a life together, long before such things were acceptable in your human society."

"You shouldn't know these things."

"I am the god of wealth, E. I can look into the mind of any person I choose and see their wealth. As well as how they got it and how they keep it."

"Handy trick," she snarked, taking another sip of her water to hide her discomfort.

"E," he called again, the command she couldn't seem to ignore in his deep voice once again. "What I am saying is I see what everyone in here does and does not wish to hide when it comes to wealth, and I can say with absolute certainty you belong here. Not because of wealth, but because of who you are."

"It's hard for me," she admitted.

His hand shot out to take hers and the touch soothed. "E, listen to me. The rich are no better than you. Many are in fact less than you."

She didn't exactly agree with him, but his words helped make her slightly less nervous. "Come, E. Let's have a lovely dinner."

"I can do that," she said, partly to answer him and partly to assure herself.

"Then we can go back to your apartment, and I can peel that delicious black dress from your body."

If she'd taken another drink of water she would've spit it out. As it was, she gawked, mouth open.

"Please, close your mouth, E. It makes me want to do wicked things."

She snapped her mouth closed. Thoughts of not belonging fled at the heat rushing over her body when she instantly imagined the wicked things he could do to and with her mouth. She no longer cared about the other people in the restaurant. She only cared about when they could leave and explore some wickedness together.

They ended up having a lovely dinner. Between random sexy comments from Plutus, they had tasty food. Except for the wagyu. She'd had American wagyu before, but they had the Japanese real deal at this restaurant and Plutus ordered it. When he offered a bit she took it, ready to be wowed. It tasted like a stick of butter in her mouth. She managed to push it down and Plutus laughed at the expression on her face. Other than that, everything had been perfect. Including Plutus.

When the waiter brought out a folio and Plutus signed something without having to even give a card, he looked over to her.

"Your place?" It might have been a question, but it felt like an assertion to her. She nodded, ready and more than willing to take Plutus home. Her body had buzzed with lust since she'd opened the door to him earlier, and she was ready to find out if the promise of him rang true.

They rushed through the restaurant and into the waiting car, his hand on her lower back the entire time, tracing maddening circles there. They didn't speak in the car, but he held her hand tight.

Plutus nearly burst from the back seat when they pulled up to her curb, dragging her along with him as he stalked up her stairs. He let her slip in front of him, but he kept close, hot on her back, as she unlocked her door.

She stumbled in but caught her feet. Only to be pushed back, back, back by Plutus. His stomp ate the ground. The tie came down and the necklace came off, transforming him in front of her eyes to the monster she'd first met in that exact spot. His horns reached high, his claws flashed on his hands, and his fangs bit down into his full lips.

Her back hit brick, and he pinned her between his massive arms, his claws tapping against the wall in a steady rhythm as he studied her face. His dipped down and he took a long, deep sniff of her neck. "You are intoxicating, E."

"Same," she breathed out.

His head came up and an eerie green light came from his eyes, so strong she saw it skim across her skin. "Tell me you want this."

"Yes. Yes, Plutus. I want this. I want you."

As soon as the last syllable was out of her mouth, his lips slammed down hard on her own. The kiss promised delightful and wicked things, maybe an edge of enjoyable pain with his pointed fangs nipping at her lips. His flexible tongue soothed the ache and pressed his advantage until she opened for him. He groaned when her tongue met his own, as if the taste of her was too much.

She knew the feeling. His taste, his smell, the sweetness of tongue and fang tore her open and gathered her up again in a new configuration. One solely concerned with pleasure.

As he scoured her mouth, one of his clawed hands moved down to her shoulder, snaking between her neck and the brick until he gripped the zipper of her dress. She leaned into him, taking more of his tongue and moaning at the feeling, as his claws lowered the zipper. The fabric gaped at her front for a second before he pulled away from her lips and tugged it down her arms and down her body, so it pooled at her pink-clad feet.

The god let out a curse, seeing her in what she thought was a simple and serviceable black cotton bra and bikini brief set. He didn't seem to care. Not as he dropped his head to lave her nipple through the fabric. Not when he dropped to his knees and used that marvelous tongue to flick over the front of her already damp panties.

"Plutus," she moaned, grabbing onto his golden horns for balance. And maybe to keep him where he was.

"Hhhhmmmm?" he teased, moving to kiss across her trembling thighs.

"Damn it," she huffed out. "I need more."

He looked up at her from his knees, his smile hungry and his eyes impossibly green and his face too beautiful for words even when she was usually so damn good with words, and she felt too wobbly to stand for a second. He must have sensed it, because he stood and scooped her up in his arms in a single heartbeat. Then they moved from the wall over to the floor, him laying her gently down on one of several lush silk cushions now littering the floor.

She didn't have time to think about where they came from, because he rose above her, tall and imposing in all his godly glory. Plutus didn't tease. He ripped off his jacket, shirt, shoes, socks, and pants, until all he had left was a tight set of gray boxer briefs that did nothing to hide the giant bulge twitching there.

E rose on her knees, licking her lips as she traced the outline with her fingers. He clamped a hand down hard on her wrist. "Oh, no, E. You do too much of that I may embarrass myself."

She pouted and he teased as he cupped his dick through his boxers. "Oh, you want it, little one? Tell me you want it."

"Please, Plutus. I want your cock."

She could've sworn she saw it jump even through the fabric, and with another broken curse, he gave her what she wanted. He kept her raised hand away and used the other hand to pull his dick from its confines.

"Oh my," was all she could say at the sight. Obviously it was big. She'd known that much from the boxer outline. What she hadn't thought about was what it might look like. And how it might be different from a human man.

The general shape was the same, sure, so no worries about it not fitting, but it would give her a good stretch. Like the rest of his skin, it glittered with what looked like gold dust. Except for his balls and head, which were solid gold, like metal made flesh. Along the shaft, he also had large, raised rings of gold melded to his flesh that looked to have tiny ridges along the outside, like a coin.

She licked her lips at the sight and he growled, dropping her wrist to grip his dick in one hand and pump it hard. "None of that, either. Not tonight."

Nope. Not tonight. What she needed then was him, deep in her, without delay. The need for it pounded in her, a rhythm she hoped like hell he'd match.

E spun around on her cushion, going down on her hands and sticking her ass in the air. She looked back at him over her shoulder and simply said, "Fuck me, Plutus."

He didn't need encouragement, apparently, because he dropped down to his own cushion and lined that golden dick up to her dripping lips. She felt a nudge then the first stretch. A hiss of pleasure left her lips, but she wanted more. Needed more.

Plutus was going too damn slow, and she tried to push back on him, but he stopped her with a clawed hand to her hip. "Still," he growled, the demand itself enough to leave her panting.

She practiced patience as he nudged and pushed, slow and sure, for agonizing minutes. Minutes he could have been fucking her, but he was being too easy. She practically clawed at the cushions in front of her by the time she felt his hips hit her ass.

"Yesss," he hissed out, and she felt him drape over her. His tongue flicked the shell of her ear and she whispered. "Brace, little one. My patience has ended."

"Thank god."

"Yes, thank me. Loudly." Then he snapped his hips back and drilled into her again with surprising speed and force. She scooted a good six inches across the floor on her cushion but he brought her back with a hard arm wrapping around her belly.

Then he fucked her.

E didn't think about much as he drove in and out. Couldn't, really. She focused on the feel of his golden cock in her, the drag and pulse of those rings around his dick. The pleasure was almost too much, and in a few short minutes her arms gave out on her, so she lowered her face to the cushion.

Plutus grabbed her hair and lifted her head up and inch to turn it to the left. "Not on your face, E," he said as he took a break from fucking her. "I want to hear those moans."

She hadn't realized how loud she'd been, or that she'd made much noise at all. "Oh, fuck, Plutus."

"That's what I'm doing," he said with a dark chuckle, and she would've laughed if he hadn't hit a spot inside her that had her cry out in bliss.

"Give. Me. Everything," he said as he smacked into her from behind. And she did. He wrung it out of her. The orgasm hit with blinding force, a subway car of pleasure taking out everything else in its wake.

She barely registered his stuttered pace, his swift exit from her. She did feel the hot seed he shot on her back with a deep grunt of pleasure. Then she collapsed on the string of pillows beneath her. Plutus fell at her side.

E turned to him and said, "We maybe should have discussed this before, but thank you for pulling out before we discussed it."

He stared at her, eyes searching her face, before he smirked. "True. Coming in you requires a talk, at the very least."

She laughed, quick and sharp, then rested her head on her arms. "I'm on birth control, as you know from the pharmacy today. I'm also clean."

"Gods don't get human diseases or infections of any kind," he offered before he grabbed a strand of her hair and started twisting it around one claw. "It's also very hard for gods to have children. Requires magic more often than not."

"Good to know those random Zeus stories aren't all true."

"Oh, they are. He's just an ass. Wait here," he whispered, before he landed a soft kiss on her forehead and padded naked down the hallway. She tried not to think too much, tried to still bask in the afterglow, and when he returned with a washcloth and cleaned her up, she also tried not to think of that.

"So, you know, if you want to, you can?"

"Hhmm?" he asked, zeroed in on the washcloth skimming her skin.

"I'm clean, you're clean. No babies likely. No more need to pull out. I don't mind. That is if, in the future, this happens again—"

His snapped up almost too quick to track. Suddenly he was all she could see. Her breath caught at the flash of pain she saw there, before the crinkle of a smirk chased it away. "I'd bet money it will happen again, little one."

She snorted, ignoring his ghost of pain. "It's not a guarantee."

"Maybe not," he purred, throwing the rag to land with a plop before his horns and handsome face came to hover over her. His searching look gave him something because he smiled, open and confident. "I'd still place the bet."

She pushed at him, his rock-solid body not budging from her shove. He did move, however, and she rose. "You're careless with money. Spend it on all kinds of frivolous things."

He leaned close into her, his voice sending shivers down her spine. "Betting on you is not such a frivolous thing."

E couldn't reply, what with the tingles starting all over again despite her very nice orgasms only minutes before. She tried to pull up anger, or at least snark, but she found something else instead. It'd been an eventful barely twenty-four hours, and she was exhausted.

Plutus scooped her up, depositing her in her small bed. He lingered at the edge of her bed a beat before he asked, "Can I sleep with you tonight?"

His green eyes, so often sure, looked vulnerable, so she nodded and scooted over toward the wall. His head dipped, his green eyes alight with thanks for some odd reason. As if she gave him some gift by letting him sleep next to her in the small double bed.

Chapter 9

E drifted out of sleep. Her body lay on the warmest mattress she'd ever felt, though it definitely wasn't the softest. Her eyes blinked open and all she saw was glittering skin. It took a second for her to register her surroundings clearly, but when her brain finally booted back online, she bolted upright, planting her hands firmly in the middle of Plutus's hard-muscled chest.

He rumbled beneath her hands, shot out his arms, and folded her snugly back against his chest. A deep sniff sounded above her head. On top of her head, actually. Absurdly, she suddenly became very self-conscious about how her hair might smell. Or if it was a matted mess of sex hair.

Oh, god, she remembered the night before. The frantic, heated, delicious sex they'd had on the floor, right where she'd summoned the god. After, when she'd agreed to let him sleep with her, he'd been far too sweet for her liking. He climbed in with her after scrounging up a bowl of ice cream. He fed her and himself, until she fell asleep curled into his warm side, the heat of him and the chill of the ice cream creating a delicious clash in her body.

Then... Damn. She'd woken up in the middle of the night, aching and needy, and reached out to him. He coaxed her on top and she'd gone willingly. Grabbing onto his tall, curved horns like they were handlebars, she'd ridden the god until she'd screamed her release at the same time as he shouted his. Again, he took care of her, carrying her to the bathroom and giving her privacy inside until he carried her back to bed once she finished cleanup. She'd slept the sleep of the truly satiated. Until then, and the idea of all of it flooded her with heat – from embarrassment and desire both.

She shouldn't be embarrassed. Had never in her sexual history felt the shyness she felt in that moment. Then again, she wasn't used to facing her sexual partners in the bright light of the morning, plastered together in her too-small-for-a-god double bed in her sad little corner of the apartment.

It was one thing to share her body, share pleasure, with a man she found attractive. Quite another to share her life—the way she lived—with them. Opening herself up to that type of judgement made her skin crawl.

However, Plutus already knew. Had known who and what she was from the jump. Spoke to something deep and tethered tight in her with his body. Even seemed to want more than her body. Plutus acted like he wanted to care for her.

Chafing at the ideas swirling in her brain, she managed to push up from his golden arms, crawl over his hulking body, and exit the bed before he snatched her up again. She beelined for the bathroom and the few minutes of peace it might give her. And maybe she did brush her teeth longer than two minutes and brush her hair for a touch too long.

When she emerged, minty-fresh and hair gleaming, she had a plan. Knew what she needed to do. She tried to ignore Plutus as she breezed into the living room, but he wasn't even there. The sound of the refrigerator door slamming made her jolt and spin. Plutus stood in the middle of the kitchen, a carton of eggs in one hand and a slab of thick cut bacon in the other. Her mouth almost watered at the sight. She loved bacon but rarely bought it because it'd gotten so damn expensive. E favored breakfast foods in general, but if she was getting some space, she needed to keep her mind set on her plan.

"Hey. I need to, uh, get going." She called this out as she scurried into her bed area. She slipped the curtain closed and dressed in shorts and a NYU t-shirt she'd gotten at grad student orientation as quickly as she could.

E flung the curtain back and Plutus was there, hovering as usual. "I have thesis work I need to get done today. At the library." The truth, at least partially. She had other things to research, too.

"You need breakfast." His voice, usually sly and joking, sounded far more rigid at this declaration.

She waved a hand and said, "I can grab coffee and a doughnut on the way." After saying it, she instinctually reached for her phone to check her bank app. To make sure she had the funds for such a pit stop. Her feet cemented to the floor, her body turned to marble in an instant, when she saw the number there.

It wasn't right, of course. There was some bank error. She'd never seen that many zeroes in a row. Five, to be exact. With a little slash of a one to cap it off. One. Hundred. Thousand.

"Shitshitshit," she muttered, her fingers flying in the app to check her deposit history. And there it was. A big honking deposit yesterday from some place she didn't recognize. Enough to get her right at the magical one hundred grand mark. She squinted down at the name of the company, her brain starting to boil. Olympus Holdings. *OLYMPUS. HOLDINGS.*

"What. Is. This?" she hissed out, turning her phone to shove the screen in Plutus's face. He seemed unconcerned, as per usual, and shrugged.

"Me upholding our bargain."

"I didn't ask–"

His smirked as her, "Oh, but you did, little one. Much like you asked me to make you come last night."

Heat rushed to her face and she couldn't tell if it was anger or embarrassment or budding lust. Likely a mix of all three. "Plutus, we talked about this."

He shook his head. "We discussed me not replacing your things. This is not replacing. It's augmenting."

E breathed in and out, steady breaths to help calm her nerves, as Plutus moved to spread out on the couch. He patted the cushion next to him, a silent invitation for him to join her, which she did not take.

Instead, she crossed her arms on her chest, cocked a hip, and prepared to let him have it. He got there first. "What I don't understand, E, is what you thought this arrangement might mean if you continue to get angry every time I fulfill a part of our bargain."

"You throwing money in my bank account was not part of our deal."

"Wasn't it? How else would I be able to make you 'comfortable' for the rest of your life?" He even used the damn air quotes at her.

She had to pause at that, because it was a good question. "I don't need this much."

Another massive shoulder shrug. "You have it. Splurge. Give it to someone else. Hell, it's yours. Do what you will with it."

She snorted. "You act like you wouldn't care, but you do. You want me to have this money."

He blinked mesmerizing, forest-canopy eyes up at her like he couldn't understand what she'd said at first. "I want you to be comfortable. As you wished. In this world, comfort most often means money."

"Money is not the only thing that can bring comfort." Now she was saying things just to argue. She needed money. It was the whole reason she called him. He gave it freely and without issue. Which, for some reason, chaffed.

He peeled off the couch, all languid grace and rippling muscle. Stopping right in her space, he looked deep into her eyes, a spark of memory flashing in his own. "Oh, I know. We offered each other much comfort last night."

E wasn't going to let him get her off track. Not that easily. Though flashes of her own memory made her more than a little wet. "We have a month together, Plutus." She said it to dig at him, remind him they were temporary. Maybe remind herself of the same. "In this month, we need to come to a more concrete understanding of expectations regarding what you should and should not do for me."

"Money is the bare minimum given our agreement, E, and you know this."

"Money isn't everything."

He shook his head. "You're right, but it helps a hell of a lot, little one. As you well know from your past."

She stiffened. He knew. Of course he did. He'd said as much the night before during dinner. He could look at a person and see their relationship to wealth, so logically he saw her lack of a relationship. Still, she hated him knowing because he would react in one of two very predictable ways.

Plutus's face softened. E found this look all too familiar and it twisted a knife in her gut.

"There is no moral failing in poverty, E, regardless of what others may have made you think in your past."

Pity it was, then.

"I don't need lectures on wealth, or lack thereof, from someone who doesn't know what it's like to do without."

His jaw clenched hard and he reached out, probably to put a beautifully veined hand on her shoulder, but she couldn't have his touch then. Couldn't bear for it to be soft and gentle and pitying like his look. "I have things to do, Plutus. A goal that has nothing to do with the accumulation of wealth, unlike some people."

The god flinched at her words, but his hand froze in midair, which was what she wanted. She scooped up her shoulder bag from the dining room table and stomped out the door. She didn't look back at Plutus. She also didn't realize she was crying until she was halfway down the block.

Within two blocks, her stomp eased and her shoulders slumped a touch. She even started feeling bad for Plutus a touch when she stopped in front of her favorite coffee spot for breakfast. A flash of anger flared when she thought of all the money she now had in her bank to pay for little luxuries, like an extra shot of espresso in her morning latte. The flare wilted when she thought of Plutus's earnest face when he told her not having money didn't affect who she was as a person.

She knew it, damnit, but a childhood being judged for where you lived and where your parents worked dug in deep. Didn't help when you spent your teens and early twenties working any job you could get in food service or retail, where people tended to crap on you constantly. Add in the way her current intern director made you feel less than because you didn't come from money, and everyone from other grad students to your advisor assume you do because they do. It was hard, dealing with others' expectations. Although she didn't like to admit it, those expectations spread like spiderwebs in her mind. She needed to dust them away, but it was hard.

Maybe Plutus could help.

The stray thought caught her up short. No. She didn't need Plutus to help with emotional labor. He was right about the monetary help. That's what she signed up for when she made her little godly bargain Friday night. Money was money. She needed to get used to it. She couldn't let herself get used to him helping her with other things.

Though, helping her out with orgasms might be nice.

She thanked the barista for the coffee and muffin, then headed out the door, sipping and trying to remain mindless for a few blocks when her blaring phone shook her from her thoughts.

"Lisa," she whispered to herself with a smile. They only talked once a week, because of the time differences and their schedules. If E hadn't called her by a certain time on a Sunday, though, Lisa always called.

E fumbled with her coffee and managed to get her phone from her bag without spilling any. Her friend's wide smile greeted her when she answered the video call.

"Hey, ho! What's up?" Lisa chirped as soon as the connection snapped into place.

"On my way to the library. What else? Any European drama to relate?"

"European drama? No. NYC drama, maybe..." She squinted at E and hit her with it. "Why didn't you go out Thursday night?"

E groaned. She'd totally forgotten about that, what with the new god in her life and all. A few of her fellow grad students had invited her out for drinks. One, she didn't have the money for it. Then. Two, she felt uncomfortable hanging out with them without Lisa around. Like she might mess up or be judged or something. Better to just say no, politely, and stay away.

"Lisa, I didn't have the time Thursday. Most days, really."

"They make time," her friend pointed out.

E sucked her teeth. She didn't want to throw money in her friend's face. Mainly because she might offer her some. She'd have needed it Thursday. Now, not so much. Thanks to Plutus.

She also didn't want to make Lisa feel bad. The grad students at NYU made her feel uncomfortable because their lives had been so vastly different. Lisa had just bulldozed over any discomfort and wormed her way in before E could realize what she was doing. E loved her, but felt no need to let anyone else in. One good friend was good, right?

"Lisa, you know I'm not great in groups."

"It was, like, five people, E."

"It's a group to me," she groused, then threw out something without thinking. Well, without thinking beyond getting her friend to ease up on her a bit. "I went out a few times this weekend."

"Ooohhh. Really? With someone?"

Panic made her heart do double-time. Shit, but she hadn't thought that through at all. She hated to lie to Lisa, but she couldn't tell her the truth, either. She decided half-truth and omission was fine for the moment. "Just had a drink Friday night and went to a museum and dinner last night."

Lisa took it the way she hoped her friend would. "It's good to get out, E, but you need people. Human interaction, you know?"

E scoffed. "Not really. Not when I have your lovely face in my life."

"Well, my face is only a screen right now. I worry about you, friend."

E's stomach dipped. She hated people worrying about her. "No need to worry. I'm lost in books, which is what I prefer. But enough of me. What fun things have popped off in London lately?"

Luckily, Lisa gave her the out, but only after a loud sigh of resignation. She told her about her past week, and E felt buoyed by the chat. She kept it up until she reached her destination and gave a rushed goodbye. Then she climbed the stone steps into the Jefferson Market Public Library.

It was a gorgeous spot. Less physical material than the main NYU library, but she didn't need physical books that day. She needed a spot Plutus wouldn't intrude on, and he knew she was a grad student at NYU. Him finding her there seemed far less likely.

She skirted the wrought-iron fence where the hidden garden bloomed and went up the sidesteps of the former church turned library. The arched doorways, stained glass, and cloistered vibe of the place gave its origins away. E liked it, though. The building had character and, despite the way sound sometimes echoed oddly because of the stone and brick structure, it was often quieter and less harried than the NYU library where she also did research. Sure, she went there when she needed to comb through the special collection. When she could do database work, like this Sunday, the large stone rooms and peaked arches worked well for her.

She circled up the rounded staircase and managed to snag a coveted back cubby in the back room of the second floor. No need to share a desk or worry about the noise echoing in the place. The small wooden table and chair even sat right in front of a thin, rectangular window overlooking the back garden, with flowers and leafy green trees blowing in the breeze. A view she could enjoy as she set about her work.

She did need to do actual thesis work, as she told Plutus. She always had thesis work she could be doing. Such was the life of a grad student. Today it was sifting through digital surveys she'd received the previous week. She'd gotten her last batch in and, after plopping the results in her massive spreadsheet, she'd finally be able to aggregate the results and think through what they all meant. She'd long ago completed the theoretical and critical sections of her thesis. The section devoted to her own work experience were done. She'd gotten her methodology finished, too. The only thing she had left to do was parse through the responses she'd received. There were a lot for qualitative library research, so she was extra proud of her participation rates. But it also meant she had a lot of opinions to comb over and interpret in light of her theoretical and experiential positions. Thankfully, she had almost two months to do it.

She managed to get the last of the survey results into her makeshift database in a little over an hour. E could start running numbers and reading written responses for common factors or ideas.

Or she could do a different type of research.

She was good at research and more than handy at a library database filled with primary sources. The perfect place for her to look for answers about a particular god who was, presumably, chilling in her apartment that very moment. She had plenty of time for surveys. Plutus was the more pressing issue.

She pulled up several databases from the NYU library site and started scouring. An hour later, she had a few answers but also new questions.

When she looked up the Greek god of wealth, she found Plutus. Not him, or at least not all the glory of him. She didn't find any images of old pottery or paintings that showed him as a massive, muscled, horned god with gold-dusted skin. Instead, there were weird representations of babies and blind dudes. Plus, there were some with wings. The baby stuff at least explained the odd, bejeweled broach of a baby he sometimes wore on his toga. There were also cornucopias everywhere he was depicted, which, fair enough. Horn of plenty and all that. Maybe that was where the horns came into play? Something to think on later.

She found out he was the son of Demeter. The idea of him having a mother, much less a goddess very famous for being a vengeful and sometimes sad mother, made her nervous. Although she did wonder what Persephone, and by extension Hades, might be like. Erasmus apparently wrote about Folly being the son of Plutus, which made her stomach churn slightly. After that, she stopped looking into family connections.

He apparently popped up in Dante's *Inferno*, which she hadn't remembered from her reading of it years ago. Reminded, she looked up Canto VII and was thrown back to a vaguely familiar debate about meaning. Dante's Plutus said the famously ambiguous line "Pape Satan, Pape Satan, Aleppo." In the epic poem, Plutus was a demon, though, not a god. Maybe the horns helped mold that representation. Still, E snorted a little at the way Plutus seemed a mystery to readers centuries later. Fitting for the sly, clever dude she met only a few days before.

Other bits and pieces filtered through, but after an hour of solid reading, she moved to her second personal research subject: *The Book of Desires*. The book brought him to her, gave her what she wanted just like the title implied, and she wanted to know more. However, there was nothing. Nada. No record she could find at least. No trace of a spell book titled *The Book of Desires*. Maybe if she contacted a local coven they could tell her more.

The idea of witches hovered in her mind for a moment. She'd cast a spell. Successfully. Anyone could *read* a spell book if they could read the language in which it was written. Not just anyone could successfully work a spell. Unless they were a witch. Mainly because of all the supernatural and humans on the planet, witches alone had access to magic.

But that wasn't true, was it? Plutus proved it false. She'd seen him, a god, perform magic in front of her. Humans didn't know gods existed, so the idea of witches having sole access to magic held for most.

All of this made her mind circle and circle. Logically, it left her with only one avenue of thought. She was either secretly a witch or a goddess. An idea she might not mind, per se, but one she'd really have to come to terms with.

Worried, she started packing up her laptop. Her back and neck hurt. She had the worst posture. A safety hazard directly related to her line of work. Throwing everything in her bag and untwisting her headphones, she hurried, head down, out of the library, wishing all the while Plutus wouldn't be there when she got home. Midway down the circular staircase, eyes downcast and lost in thought, she moved to the side when she heard another person ascending the stairs in front of her. Only they didn't pass in the narrow gap. They stopped, looming large before she could even look up. They purred, "Looks like your work is done, little one."

Guess Plutus wasn't in her apartment after all. E really needed to be far more mindful about the wishes she made.

Chapter 10

E's breath left her like she'd been hit hard in the chest. Partially from the surprise of Plutus showing up in the cool, dark spiral staircase when she didn't expect him to be there. Partially because he was so damn beautiful.

Even human, he looked intimidating, with that bronzed skin, height, and bulk. He loomed in the tight space, but the cocky smirk on his lush mouth made him less frightening. She looked over this face, a part of her sad because she missed the golden cast of his skin and his horns when he hid himself.

"E?" He asked, concern melting over his face as she looked at him like some star-struck dummy. He reached out, hands moving to her waist as if to steady her or pull her close. She wanted both. The jolt of his hands on her, the now-familiar zap and pull of him, helped her once again find her voice.

"I'm good, Plutus. Just a little startled. How did you find me?"

The smirk came back, slow and sensual as he looked her over. "Were you trying to hide from me, little one? Not going to work. I can find you anywhere." She opened her mouth to ask more about it, but he held up his hand. "Are we playing our question game?"

E quickly shook her head. She'd done enough research she now had a basis to form some real hard-hitting questions for him, so she wasn't about to waste one when she didn't know where it might lead.

He chuckled. "Thought not. Come." He dropped his hands from her waist after a quick squeeze and grabbed her left hand. Her palm fit perfectly in his, and she thought next time he was in his true form, she wanted to hold his clawed hand and see if there was a difference.

"We are going to…" She trailed off to make it ambiguous. She didn't want him smacking her with a question tax for something so basic.

"Back to your apartment. I'm making you dinner."

At the mention of food, her tummy rumbled, loud as any growl she'd heard from Plutus. She blushed in embarrassment as Plutus cut hard eyes back at her, not minding the twisting stairs at all but keeping his feet steady. "Did you eat lunch?"

"Are we playing our question game?"

They reached the bottom of the stairs and he tugged her arm hard. Not enough to hurt, but enough to send her off balance, tumbling into his tight arms. He held her close, and with one large hand tilted her chin up so she could look into his brilliant, serious eyes. "You will take care of yourself."

"So bossy," she groused, but it was hollow. Mostly because she was panting at their closeness, even in public.

His hand moved from her chin to her cheek then into her hair, tilting her head back more and giving a delicious tug. "I can show you bossy if you like."

Her legs nearly buckled at the steel of his deep voice and she found herself whispering "yes" before she realized it. It was like her mouth, or more likely her pussy, bypassed her damn brain.

Plutus smiled then, big and wolfish. No smirk in sight. "As you wish, little one." He steadied her on her feet before grabbing her hand once again and leading them out into the bright light of a Sunday afternoon in the Village.

Plutus cooked her dinner, as promised. E did nothing, which was nice. Plutus brought her a glass of wine so red and smooth it had to be expensive as hell, but she refused to ask. If she didn't know for sure, she couldn't feel awkward about it. She'd managed to not admit she'd been wrong that morning about things, mainly because she'd kept her mouth mostly shut.

He'd taken off his necklace once they were inside, so he was in full monster form. E giggled a bit when she noticed his tall horns almost skimmed the ceiling. And Lisa had high ceilings.

Her giggle made Plutus cut his eyes to her. She pointed to the top of his head. "You're almost too tall."

"We need to spend some time in my apartment," he muttered. "I have much higher ceilings for this very reason."

She froze, thinking about being in his space and what she might learn there without even having to play their little game. He took her silence as a question. "I have an apartment in the building we went to the other night. Which is how I got us the reservation. No magic required."

She spun back around on the couch, facing away from him, and took a big old gulp of her wine. That small section of the city, where huge skyscraper apartments faced Central Park, was known as Billionaire's Row for a reason. Maybe he'd magicked ownership of the apartment, but it didn't even matter. He had it. Owned it, likely. Which meant he was property rich to an extent she couldn't even imagine. And she lived in a one-bedroom second floor walkup in Greenwich Village. Had seen Lisa and her parents spend money in a way she found uncomfortable. Because she'd never been comfortable with money. Then here was Plutus, throwing around money and magic for her. Giving her so much so quickly while also short-circuiting her body with his tingles and tongue and lovely monster peen.

She took another deep drag of wine, draining the glass this time. Thankfully, Plutus gave her room to think, humming softly to himself as he sautéed something in her kitchen. E knew her reactions were based in trauma, in a life where monetary survival hung by a thread at times. Like when she called up Plutus to begin with. He offered her all she needed. Wanted to give her so much more than she needed. Hard to trust, though, when she'd never been able to rely on someone to offer her security in this way. Not her family, not even herself. It was an odd, warring mix of shame, hyper-independence, and desire for what she'd never had that made her hesitant with Plutus. At least with her feelings and needs. E'd given her body, and would again. She didn't know if she could give more, and with all Plutus was offering, she wasn't sure if it was fair.

Plutus rumbled from the kitchen, "Dinner will be ready in five. Set the table, please."

Thankful for a task to take her out of her heavy thoughts, she jumped up and scooped up the plates, linens, and silverware he'd piled up on one of the counters. She looked it over as she set it. E'd asked Lisa how to set a formal table. She'd been to a few formal dinner parties with the department and wanted to make sure she didn't embarrass herself. Lisa'd gone out and bought all these trappings, which they really didn't need, just to help E understand and feel better. She'd been choked up when Lisa came in with huge, heavy bags from the West Elm a few blocks over. Thinking back now at the generosity she struggled with when it came to her best friend, she could see how she was doing the same to Plutus, though she was a little more aggressive with it. Both deserved better than her, with all her hangups.

"Hey," she heard whispered behind her before large, clawed hands hugged her belly from behind. E breathed deep, in and out, and shook her head.

"Sorry. Lost in thought for a sec," she said, trying to ease the worry she heard in his voice. He spun her in his arms, cocooning her in the golden muscles and claws so she felt warm and safe, and looked her over. He nodded after a moment, likely not believing her but giving her the out she needed, nonetheless.

"I'll be out with food in a moment," he said. Then, he dipped down quickly and planted a firm, sweet kiss in the middle of her forehead. Her heart fluttered, but he turned away before she could say or do anything.

Sighing at the mixed signals her own brain was throwing at her, she set the table as Lisa taught her over a year ago, placing the last fork when Plutus came up behind her. She looked up, a hesitant and expectant smile on her lips, and he said "Beautiful." With his eyes trained only on her, she thought he might not mean the table.

"Thanks," she said, not asking for clarification, because she had other questions.

Plutus plated their dinner, a beautifully cooked salmon with some type of glaze on a pile of veggies and fragrant rice. They took their seats and Plutus explained it was miso glaze and jasmine rice. Then silence fell for a few minutes as both dug in. E wolfed down her food, the smells making her hungrier than she'd been all day. Plutus ate slowly, more deliberately, staring at E across the table all the while.

When she shoveled half of the food in, her hunger eased and she was able to focus on conversation. After a large bite she asked, "Would you like to play twenty questions?"

He nodded and flashed his fangs. "Sure."

"Okay then." She steadied herself and went with her first question. She'd meticulously planned three questions to ask him this evening. "I'll go first. How are you related to Demeter?"

Plutus set his fork down on his plate and leaned back in his chair. "I see you did some research into me today. It shouldn't be surprising, but I do wonder what exactly you read." There was a long pause as he looked down at his plate. Seemingly making some decision, he nodded to himself and looked back to E.

"Demeter is my mother, as you probably found. Which means, yes, Persephone is my sister and Hades is my brother-in-law. They're all far more famous than I am, especially these days, but they are my immediate family. You likely also heard I have a son. However, he is my adopted son. I'd very much like you to meet him, all of them, one day. Along with my best friend, Boreas, who recently found his own ma– woman."

He twisted slightly in his seat, as if uncomfortable about something, and cleared his throat before he continued. "The Greek gods are all real, all interconnected, and most of them still live, taking more of a place in this world than others. However, all are secret to humans. As you may have guessed after the vampire incident outside the club, other supernatural beings know we exist. They sense our power and magic easily, so it would be too difficult to hide away from them. Plus, they themselves hid for so long. We often helped one another back then."

She thought he was done with his story because he picked up his fork as if he would take a bite of food. He didn't. He pushed rice around his plate for a beat then said, "We were hunted. Killed, when humans discovered gods were not immortal, just long-lived. When some of us pushed too hard down on the humans who worshipped us."

E gasped. She knew, as all humans did, of the bloody and horrible history of the supernatural reveal hundreds of years ago. She could imagine a similar thing happening further back in time, pushing gods to hide themselves. She focused back on Plutus. "We decided, as a whole, to hide from human society. They had reason to hate and distrust us. Even if many of us never mistreated them, too many had abused their power. Forced the human's hand, really." Shaking his head as if to shake out dark memories, he said. "You are now one of only a few humans who know who I am, who my family is."

He didn't appear sad or hesitant about the fact, as if he trusted her. Sure, E knew she'd never tell anyone about Plutus. No one would believe her anyway, but more than that, she wouldn't hurt Plutus that way. Something in her gut twisted like a hot knife when she considered the idea of him hurting in any way. Enough she gently shoved her plate away, her appetite disappearing all of a sudden.

Plutus, forehead wrinkled and eyebrows turned down, said, "E, please eat. I wanted to give you this, let you know who and what I am, to some extent. There is no reason to lose your appetite over it. My family isn't that bad."

She snorted out a laugh. "I'll take your word for it." A claw hovered in her view as she stared down at her plate, clicking one, two, three times until she pulled it back to where it had rested in front of her and picked up her fork.

He let her eat a few bites before he said. "My turn." She braced and he asked, "You now know some things about my immediate family. What's your immediate family like?"

"Oh, you know, regular human family." When he gave her a hard stare, she sighed. "My father works at one of the few factories left in my tiny Ohio town, though that steady job is new to him. He was in and out of work for most of my childhood. My mother is a waitress and has been my whole life. Worked at the same small, family-owned diner for decades."

"You've told me their vocations when I asked what they were like," Plutus said pointedly before putting a flaky chunk of salmon in his mouth.

Another sigh left E. "Well, their jobs are important. They're small-town people with hard jobs who've scraped to get by their whole lives. They live in the same single-wide trailer they lived in my whole childhood. They do the same things and see the same people. Nothing much changes for them because they don't have much room to change."

"But their daughter changed."

"Yes. Their only child moved away, left them to it, so she could do something else."

"I imagine they are proud of you."

She nodded. "Of course they are, and they say it, but my life and their life are vastly different now, and will be from here on out."

"And you feel guilt over it."

"Sure do. Only a monster wouldn't feel guilty leaving them behind when they worked so hard for so long for me, right?" The question slipped out in frustration and she wished she could bite it back. For wasting a question and for what it revealed about her.

Plutus waved away the question he didn't answer. He wouldn't answer because it wasn't part of their game. "You are a good daughter, E."

"You can't know that, Plutus."

"I know guilt only comes to those who care. Believe me, I deal with plenty of people who would never feel such guilt because they are not good people."

Ready to get out of this conversation, she turned it on him. "My question again. How did I summon you?"

He laughed at the abrupt change in topic but went with it. "Only witches and gods can summon, as they are the only beings who can perform magic."

"I'm a witch." E stated it as if it were now fact. Then, her face flashed with awe and she whispered, "Or am I a god?"

A big belly laugh rumbled out of him, and she watched him laugh so hard tears fell from his bright green eyes. "No, little one. No. You have no magic." She waited for him to stop laughing so he could give her more. "*The Book of Desires* was created by Hecate and a witch, directed at giving hidden gods… something they might need. I performed a spell in the book centuries ago, which is what brought me to you. You found the book, or more aptly, the book found you, so my spell could be completed."

They stared at each other a few beats. His answer raised more questions, but she wasn't going to waste any. He usually gave her more than necessary, but not this time. He arched an eyebrow her way, waiting for follow up questions that never came. Well, damn. She got something but not enough. She'd need to rethink and regroup. At least she now knew she wasn't a secret witch.

"Me again." He propped his chin up on his closed fist, a perfect imitation of The Thinker, before he asked, "What's your favorite dessert?"

E sucked her teeth a moment. Looked like he wasn't going to get deep again. "Yellow cake with chocolate icing. Especially if it's boxed cake and tub icing."

He nodded and muttered "I can do that." The idea of him making her cake brought a true smile to her face, but also brought the third question she'd ask tonight to the front of her mind.

Her smile faded and she whispered "You have everything. Seem comfortable in the city. Even have your own apartment here. What are you getting out of this arrangement?"

"I told you. Time."

"But...?" She trailed off, again stopping the questions.

He answered her unasked question this time. "Time with you is enough for me. Will always be enough. I have much, E. I do not have someone like you in my life."

Her gut thumped. Like the thing she knew connected them strummed in pleasure at his words. MINE flashed, hot and insistent, across her mind but she brushed it aside, something to think on later. Much later. She just nodded at what he said and let silence fall.

"Okay, final question, before dinner is over. Will you allow me to give you a gift, little one?"

"Oh, Jesus," she said, hanging her head. She hated getting gifts, especially when there wasn't equity in the relationship. Hence her fit over the laptop and phone. But he asked, and he'd been so sweet, and he looked so expectant. She couldn't let disappointment flit across his face, not after her tantrum that morning and how he'd let her have it without explanation or apology.

"Yes," she managed to get out. Then, she clarified. "You may give me one, singular, gift."

A smile stretched wide, uncovering his fangs, and he said, "One moment," before he leapt up to get something out of the coat closet by the door. Whatever it was, he was real happy about it. Excited even. She dreaded it, more than a little, but told herself to grit her teeth and bare it. For Plutus, and all he'd done for her, all he'd told her, so far.

Chapter 11

Plutus came back from the coat closet dangling a Burberry shopping bag from his hand. He set it on the side of the table, out of the way of the fishy plates, of course, then sat himself back down across from her.

"I may have noticed your work bag appeared a little frayed, and I may have gotten you something to replace it."

"It's just that easy for you, with your magic and all." There was no heat or venom in her words. She wasn't jealous, exactly. More like sad about how easy some had it when she'd been using said frayed bag for years now because she couldn't justify the expense when it still technically worked.

Plutus sat up straight and sucked his teeth. "I did not 'magic' this bag into existence, E. My magic allows me to access wealth and luxury, not create it out of thin air."

She quirked an eyebrow at him and he waved off her concern about asking questions. "Our game is over. For now. I will give you free rein to ask about this because I think it might be beneficial for us both."

Almost giddy with excitement over the chance to ask him any number of questions, she blurted out as many as she could at once. "How does your magic work, exactly? Do you take these things or spirit them away or something? How does it work with money and all the cash you put in my bank account? Do you just take whatever you want?"

Plutus narrowed his jade eyes at her and addressed each and every one, his tone becoming a little harsher with each answer. "Godly magic is an affinity. I can use other, smaller magic, but all the major magic I perform must connect with wealth in some way, shape, or form. This means I can read the minds and desires of humans, but only as it pertains to wealth or money. No human can stop me from accessing wealth or knowledge of it, and I have a natural ability to correctly judge business ventures and investments. I can take wealth or provide it on a case-by-case basis. I do not, however, steal."

"I didn't mean–"

He held up a hand and E stopped her excuse mid-sentence. That's what it was. She was so excited to ask him anything without cost she'd inadvertently accused him of stealing.

"Millenia ago, I doled out punishments and rewards, but others doing such things, those with mighter and more powerful fists, led to our downfall, so I learned that lesson well. I do not do such now."

"Do I use my affinity to help those I find deserving? Yes, when I find them. I also use it to give myself and those I love legitimate human wealth in this society." He smirked and looked off, as if thinking of something funny to himself before hitting her with what she now considered his trademark cocky smirk. "I do very well in the stock market."

Plutus spread his hands wide, "I have no need to steal because I have earned more than enough wealth over the years. I do not punish, as unfair as it seems to me at times, because the cost of being an arbitrator of humans is far too great. A few days ago, I did 'magic' a few things for you because I felt you needed them immediately. However, I credited all accounts and, in the case of your new wardrobe and the tech you didn't take, I had a personal shopper in another region purchase them and then made them appear here, which I see could be a little questionable or confusing in your mind because you didn't know. I went to the Burberry store this afternoon and purchased this bag with my very own credit card."

E hated being in the wrong, but especially in this, Plutus's hard voice exposed his hurt. "I'm sorry my questions were so insensitive."

"Apology accepted," he said. After a beat, with a wide grin, he added, "as long as you now open your gift."

E let out a breath. She knew the brand of course, knew it was expensive, but didn't know how expensive. She'd let it go, though, because she said she would. Because Plutus went out personally and picked it out for her.

She dug through the tissue paper until she lifted out a large, rectangular leather shoulder bag. The embossed pattern on the outside created a sort of single-color plaid on the leather. The feel of it was supple, soft. It was such a deep black it seemed to suck up the light. When she breathed in, it smelled earthy and rich. She unzipped the bag and it didn't stick or snag like her bag sometimes did. Inside was silky soft fabric with plenty of room for her laptop, a few books, notebooks, and her rotating but endless supply of pens. Truly, a perfect bag. Simple but obviously expensive in feel and craftsmanship, even if someone missed the small, embossed logo on the top of one side of the case.

Plutus let her explore all this as he explained his choice. "It's understated and will work with whatever you might wear. Wherever you may go, now and in the future. You may need to treat the leather, but the material will shelter your books and things so they stay safe and secure. Technically, it's a man's briefcase, but this one seemed far more fitting and practical for you than any of the women's bags, which didn't have as much room or had open tops so things might get damaged if it rained." When she didn't say anything to his explanation, in a softer voice he added, "If you don't like it..."

"No..." she started, but had to clear her throat to dislodge the odd lump there before she could continue. "No. It's perfect. What I might pick out if I were there."

Plutus seemed to sit straighter at the words, as if he cared about knowing what she would like. As he'd given her so much already, even just this night, she thought she could give him a little more. "I'm not good at taking gifts, for a lot of reasons, but this is truly a great gift, Plutus, and I will use it for a very long time."

He leaned close, almost reaching across the table with his torso, and purred, "I like the idea of you having a piece of me with you for a good, long time."

She laughed. "A bag isn't you, Plutus."

He retreated and shrugged. "The bag, no. The gift, yes. All gifts are a little piece of the giver. Or, at least, a glimpse into what the giver thinks of or thinks is important to the recipient."

The pesky lump was back, but the heat in her blood flared at his words, at what he thought of her, if she took his words to heart. Instead of revealing more, she rose from her seat, slid around the table, and bent to take Plutus's lips with her own. She offered up a hungry kiss, one meant to stoke and stroke. He had no problem taking the gift she offered him, but he did stop her after a delicious minute. "Move to the couch, E." The hard edge of his voice, the command, made her think of what he said earlier, and she knew she was in for a very good time with a bossy god.

She moved, a jerky and admittedly wet mess, as she heard him move behind her, turning out lights until one corner lamp and the soft yellow glow of the hall light illuminated the apartment. She sat, butt barely on the edge of the couch, hands fidgeting in her lap from her excited energy. "Calm," he commanded from her right. Plutus sauntered over, and the new lighting created the perfect glint of gold off his molten skin.

"You're beautifully blinding," she breathed out, unable to stop the words. She didn't think men liked to be called beautiful, but she'd said it, so it lay out there in the middle of the room with them.

The god didn't seem to mind. Quite the opposite. He stopped in front of her, snagging her chin firmly and lifting her head up so he could look down on her with those glowing green eyes of his. He smiled, a soft one she'd never really seen on him yet, and stroked her right cheek with a single claw in a caring gesture. Then the softness turned to a tilt of his lips and the claw dug in a touch too sharp.

"Speaking of beautiful..." His clawed thumb dug into her left cheek, both sharp points now nudging insistently where each side of her jaw hinged. "Open for me, E."

She let her mouth fall open, sticking out her tongue without being asked to do so. A deep, dark growl rumbled up from him. Without moving his hand or breaking eye contact, he unzipped his trousers and pulled out his glistening cock. The head shone with precum and it twitched as she caught sight of it. The metallic sheen and embossed golden rings gleamed before her, a sweet, heady offering.

Plutus moved his hand from her face to gather up her pink hair and hold it tight at the back of her head. "Suck me, E."

She didn't need to be told twice. Like a thirsty woman offered a golden goblet, she sipped greedily. As soon as he passed her lips, the tarnish coin taste of him flooded her mouth, making it water. He was smoke and old coins and the barest hint of expensive whiskey and she wanted to drink it all in deep.

Her tongue swirled over his head, teasing for a long minute. When she bobbed down enough to hit the first and smallest raised ring, the tip of her tongue traced the edge, gliding the small ridges she loved inside her so much. The exploration left her giddy, almost drunk with pleasure, and achingly wet. This slow progress, however, was not enough for the god and he nudged the back of her head. A demanding grunt sounded from above her as she raised her eyes up while keeping her mouth fully engaged. "I said suck it, not tease it," he hissed.

She offered him a look she hoped came off as sexy and seductive and not just hungry and engulfed the first few inches of length in her mouth. She sucked, hard, as she roamed the length up and down with her tongue. Every so often, she took more. And more. And more into her mouth. Until she couldn't take any more. Sadly, there were still a few inches and raised rings left, so she clamped a hand down on the remaining length, twisting it as she bobbed her head up and down on Plutus's lovely, golden cock.

"Shit, E. Yeah. Just like that, baby. Suck me down deep. As deep as you can."

Plutus let her have control for several minutes, until he gripped her wrist and pulled her hand from his length. She looked up with wide eyes and he growled. "Swallow for me, little one."

At first she thought he was coming, but nope, he started pumping into her mouth, gentle but at a steady pace, pushing through her gentle gags. He wanted her to swallow his tip so he could fuck her throat. Not something she'd done before, but she was so horny and achy she'd give anything a try if he commanded her to do so.

After a minute of trying, she felt his head slip past a tight ring of muscles and he cursed loud and long, stroking into her throat for several long beats. Not enough to cut off her air too long, but enough for her to feel heady for taking so damn much of him at once.

He slipped free of her throat, then her mouth, pumping with his hand as he wiped away some of the mess he'd made of her mouth. "Beautiful," he growled before he again demanded, "Open for me." She did, same as before, wide and tongue out. His dick slid in with ease and he stroked it in and out in quick succession, until he shouted his release. She swallowed it all, sucking it deep, and wished there was more of the smoky, musky goodness with just the hint of metallic taste.

His grasp on her head eased and he reached into his pocket, pulling free a pristine white handkerchief. Crouching in front of her, not even bothering to put his dick away first, he cleaned her face as best he could and cooed over her. "Good girl," he said, and she nearly preened for him.

Standing again, he gestured, "Now lay back for me, along the length of the couch." E did as she was told, landing with her head on the armrest. He wasted no time nudging his large shoulders between her legs so one fell over his shoulder and the other dangled off the sofa. He nipped at her thighs through her shorts then tongued her through them. Despite the multiple layers between them, she jolted at the contact. Plutus growled, took the button of her shorts between his large fangs, and ripped it clean off.

"Hey! I like these," she protested, though it sounded a little too breathy to be much of a deterrent after the fact.

"Means I get to buy you a new pair," he quipped, then pinned her with both a hot, strong hand and his green gaze. "Now shut up, lie back, and let me eat my dessert."

E wasn't about to argue with that, so she did what she was told as he slipped the tattered shorts and intact panties down over her ass and hips so he had access to her pussy. He scented her, rubbing his nose so close to her slit she felt his breath. "I'm starved for you," he said before a single claw came up, spread her wide, and his long, snaking tongue took a lick from top to bottom.

That deliciously nimble tongue flicked hard over her clit before slithering down to dip deep into her dripping opening. The rest was a blur of need and want and moans. He urged on every sound she made, eventually bringing a claw into play so he could rub her clit with the smooth outer gold as he tongue-fucked her, pausing only to scrape her gently with a fang at unpredictable intervals. She keened whenever he switched from claw-on-clit to moving his claw deep inside with expert precision so he didn't cut or scrape. The play between sharp and soft ratcheted, what he could do and what he chose to do, for her, ratcheted up her need.

"Look at you take me so well, little one. Your tiny, perfect pussy is just greedy for my claws and fangs. My greedy little thing." He gently nipped her clit with one of his fangs and she screamed, the small slice of pain causing every other delicious feeling to heighten.

"Please. Please. Please." She called out for him to keep going, keep pushing, like a benediction. Like a prayer. The god answered with a hard suck on her nub and a perfectly timed twist and slide of two fingers inside her and she exploded into a million tiny fragments. Her legs twitched uncontrollably even as she felt the wave of pleasure crest and crash down.

Plutus watched her aftershocks hit with a satisfied smirk on his face. When E started stirring on the couch, rolling around as if she'd get up, he stilled her with a stiff arm to her chest. "Oh, no, little one. We're not done yet."

He moved too quickly for her to register, jumping to his feet and scooping her into his arms in one swift motion. She didn't squirm as he stalked to her little bedroom alcove. To her bed. Where she knew he'd give her more of everything she wanted.

Chapter 12

She figured she eventually fell asleep, because she woke up wrapped in Plutus' heavy, claw-tipped arms. She came to all warm and snuggly and safe feeling, until she realized the blare of her preset work alarm sounding from the living room was what woke her.

"Shitshitshit," she muttered to herself before she heard a loud oomph from behind her. In her rush to get clear of Plutus and her bed, she'd accidentally elbowed him in his stomach. She thought he should be able to take it, what with his general god strength and all those abs, but she still threw out a "sorry" as she scrambled to her feet.

In ten minutes, she was done with the bathroom, her teeth brushed, makeup light, and hair pulled back in a manageable pink pony. E stripped out of her pajamas as carefully as possible so as not to waste the quick work she just did then threw on a crisp white button up and buttery-soft gray slacks from the clothes haul Plutus gave her what felt like ages ago.

"Why so frantic, little one?" Damn, but his morning rough voice, somehow even deeper than his regular deep voice, made her core quiver. But no time for that.

She sat on the bed as she pulled out a shoebox to find a pair of shiny patent leather ballet flats with, once again, a tell-tale bloody bottom. With no time to think about the mass of money now in her closet, she turned her head to look over at a rumpled and sexy af monstrous god stretched across her bed.

"I have work this morning at my internship. Then an afternoon meeting with my academic advisor about my thesis. And I left my phone in the living room last night after-"

"My dessert," he purred, knifing up quickly to trial kisses along the side of her scarred neck as if he didn't notice the light pink ghosts of burns past.

"Ugh, yes," she whined out before she managed to shove him away. "None of that. Not now, anyway. I'm already running late because it took me forever to hear the alarm from under all that muscle this morning. If the bus is behind or anything I'm for sure late."

He cocked a head at her in question then said, "The car is downstairs waiting for you." His tone sounded as if she were the one being absurd. How was E supposed to know he'd have a fancy car service at her beck-and-call?

"No time to argue about it. Actually, I won't argue about it. It's a good thing this morning." She jumped up only to spin and bend deep into the bed to give Plutus a quick but thorough kiss. "Thank you."

Luckily, with her happiness over Plutus's gift for her the night before, she'd transferred all her stuff from her old bag after he sexed her up in bed. Stuffing her phone and her extra charger in the thing before zipping it closed, she called out "Later" before she slammed the apartment door shut.

Thank the god (who she suspected was responsible), the very kind driver had a steaming cup of strong coffee in his hand, passing it off to her as he opened the back door. She felt weird, being surrounded by the leather luxury of the backseat without Plutus by her side, but she pushed it out of her mind in favor of plunking her head against the soft seat and resting there for the duration of her ride, sipping the luscious coffee along the way.

The driver managed to make it uptown in record time and she rushed into her workstation with a few minutes to spare.

"E," Anne chirped, a jaunty wave and smile ready for her. She stood close to Mitchel, not far from her desk.

Her boss gave her an up-and-down. Not abnormal, except his gaze snagged and locked on the bag slung across her shoulders. When she slipped free from the bag and plopped it down on her desk, the soft thump of it shook off his look. With clipped, assured steps, he came over to her desk, a saccharine smile on his lips. Something she didn't really need given her rather frantic morning, but he was her boss so she couldn't exactly tell him to leave her the hell alone. Instead, she managed to say, "Good morning, Mitchel," like a respectable adult.

"Edith." He said, shitty and formal as always. A little shorter than normal but not unheard of from Mitchel. He reached up to adjust his tie before he said, "Have an enjoyable weekend?"

"I did."

He nodded and hummed some non-committal noise in reaction. His hand left his tie and smoothed over her bag; his touch weirdly intimate on the leather. E's body lurched in automatic reaction, both from the idea and the fact of him touching something of hers. Something Plutus gave her. She just managed to tamp down the urge to snatch the bag away.

"Interesting new briefcase, Edith." She said nothing, and he looked up, pinning her in place with cold eyes. "Rather interesting, and expensive, given you asked for a raise only days ago."

Of course he knew it was a luxury bag. He probably had one just like it in his closet. E shrugged. "It was a gift."

"Umm-hmm," he said, still staring. "I'm sure."

What the hell did that even mean? She figured he had some idea about the working poor now confirmed by her expensive bag, like she got government assistance to buy luxury items or something. Asshole. She crossed her arms at her chest and tapped her foot, which brought his gaze down. He smirked (not in a sexy Plutus way) but he said nothing. Mitchel turned on his heels without a word and strolled from the work room, off to hide in his barely lit office and leave the real work to the peons he oversaw.

"Yeesh," Anne said, taking his place in front of E, though she looked behind her at where Mitchel just disappeared.

"What's his problem?"

"Oh, it's probably me," Anne said. "I came in early to tell him about the missing book. I mean, he gave it to me and it poofed, so I thought he should know. It's still not in the database. He had some excuse about wonky IT issues and other missing entries when he locked onto you for whatever reason. As always, his actions are a mystery, just like the missing book."

"Yeah, a mystery," E mumbled, looking away from the woman. She of course knew the answer to one of those mysteries: where *The Book of Desires* was.

As for the other mystery, she didn't give a damn, unless it meant more random weirdness from Mitchel.

"Oh, well," Anne said, her sunny personality coming back through as she toyed with the beaded chain dangling from the arms of her glasses and looping around her neck. "Mondays, am I right?"

E snorted and nodded and the woman moved back to her workstation. Sitting at her own desk, E pushed thoughts of the "missing" book and odd boss out of her head so she could focus on the actual book in front of her, or the pamphlets she was trying to free from the book binding in front of her. Whatever Mitchel's deal, she didn't have time for it.

"You've done truly excellent work so far," Dr. Hamilton said after taking a little too long to look over what E'd recently written as E sat there awkwardly.

E liked her academic advisor well enough. Respected her very much, especially as a woman who'd been in the field for decades. However, Dr. Hamilton was often a little late in reading her work. She also dismissed her financial needs, as if rigorous academic study by itself could pay the bills.

Still, despite the occasional awkwardness, E learned a lot from her, so she looked forward to their talks about her work. "Thank you," E said. "I've basically finished everything but the distillation of my last surveys. Once I've combed through the data, I can craft my last section, and hopefully be finished."

Dr. Hamilton leaned back in her chair, nodding her head so her thick, straight gray bob bounced around her head. "I see no problem with your timeline. Your methodology is sound, your understanding of the literature impeccable. If you give yourself the proper time to peruse the data and reach your conclusions, you will be fine."

E's jaw tightened at the last line. It was a favorite of Dr. Hamilton's. The professor probably thought it was comforting, but it grated on E. "You'll be fine" always sounded dismissive of her worries and fears.

Dr. Hamilton continued. "I wished to talk about one more topic with you this afternoon." E sat, still and silent, unsure what would come next. You never knew what might happen. "I recently sent my evaluation of your graduate work to the head of Special Collections at Ohio State. Glowing, of course, as you deserve. Yet, I wonder if this is really what you wish to do."

"What do you mean?"

"Well, to be frank, I think you have the potential to be more. You have a bright mind and a tenacious work ethic. I think you should consider continuing with your graduate studies."

"Like get a PhD?"

"Yes. It is sadly a little late for you to apply for this coming academic year's cohort, but I believe your application would do well given the current graduate committee. You would most certainly be offered admittance for the following year. Maybe even with a stipend."

The "maybe even with a stipend" hurt. E managed to just barely hold back the flinch. Would she like to spend her days studying with other like-minded people, talking old books all day? Sure. However, she wasn't in a position to do more graduate education she couldn't afford. Then she remembered Plutus's little deposit in her account. Actually, she could freely study all she wished. Well, for at least the four to five years it'd take her to get a PhD. If she also had the stipend. Who even were these people who could do graduate school without stipends? And how out of touch was Dr. Hamilton with E's own history to think it would be an option?

"I greatly appreciate the recommendation and I'll consider your thoughts on my future here more. I have several more months before applications are due, correct?"

"Yes, yes. Practical as always, Ms. Micheals. Finish the work in front of you before committing to more in the future." Dr. Hamilton turned back to her laptop, clicking through a few things before she looked up again. "I suggest we meet one final time early next month to go over the data and what you have written up this far. It would then give you a few weeks to finish writing up the results, do any final revisions on your thesis, then present it to your committee in plenty of time for an August graduation. I'll even petition for you to walk in August prior to your defense."

"Plenty of time" might be pushing it, when such a timeline would only give her a week or two buffer for the deadline for graduation, but she knew she could do it. The thought of walking across the huge stage, kneeling in front of Dr. Hamilton, made her heart race with both nerves and excitement. It was the big symbolic end to all this work and worry. "Thank you," she said, meaning it with her whole heart.

Dr. Hamilton nodded her acknowledgement of the thanks and they then worked out a specific date and time for their next thesis talk. After, E felt both stressed and elated, a peculiar sensation she'd gotten used to while in graduate school. She loved learning, loved talking about what she learned with others who also loved learning, but there was a whole lot of pressure that came along with that luxury. Add in the money issues—but she didn't have those money issues anymore. Which left her with a singular question: did she want to do all this over again or did she want to move on and start her career?

Big, heady question she'd have to mull over another time, because she spotted Plutus, in his human guise, leaned against the car, waiting at the curb for her.

"How long've you been here?"

"Only a few minutes. No need to worry about me blocking the loading zone just for you." He winked at her as he opened the door and waited for her to scoot inside. He climbed in after her and as soon as the door closed behind them, the driver shot off.

"So you don't have to ask," he said to her with a green twinkle in his eyes, "I have no concrete plans for this afternoon. I thought we could do whatever you wished to do."

She thought for a moment and spoke. "I want a good cocktail. And a slice of cake."

Plutus's smile widened. "I think we can manage that." He rolled down the divider and told the driver to take them to some address up around Midtown. She trusted him to know where she could get a good drink and a tasty piece of cake. But to be honest, she'd be just as happy eating him up. She wasn't about to tell him that, though. She knew they'd get there at some point in the day, anyway, what with the way they seemed to crash together whenever they were alone. E decided a little luxury sure was nice, and let Plutus take the lead with a quiet but comfortable car ride to liquor and dessert.

Chapter 13

E downed an espresso martini and a fluffy angel food cupcake with the lightest buttercream she'd tasted in her life. Plutus may have growled at her halfway, but only because she kept moaning around bites of the thing. She giggled and promised to control herself. "Don't say such a thing, little one. I like when you lose control. Maybe just tamp down the moans in public. For my sanity."

She managed it, and they enjoyed conversation in the midtown restaurant. E told him about the weirdness with Mitchel. The curl of his lips at the mention of her boss made her laugh. He didn't even know anything about the man. "I dislike him on principle alone," he replied when she pointed out the fact. Fair enough, in her mind. But only because she did know the man and he deserved the god's dislike.

She told him about her advisor meeting with much more enthusiasm. He sat across from her, occasionally twisting his martini glass and adding encouraging words and sounds as she talked about her thesis work.

E asked about his day, and he talked about a conversation he had with his sister, the business calls he had to take, and some deliveries he had to pick up at his apartment. "Speaking of which," he eased into the conversation. "I would like you to come to my apartment with me after this."

She knew it wasn't far, since he'd told her they'd gone to the restaurant in his building. She also knew she had to get over her hangup connected to his wealth. He was the god of wealth. He'd also explained his magic and how he used it last night, so she needed to let him be more open with it and what he'd gotten with it. His power was who he was in many ways.

She lifted a shoulder as if it were no big deal when she was more than a little nervous about it all. "Sure. No problem."

He snorted at her feigned indifference, but let her have it, giving her a little space as he called for and then paid the check.

He stood, straightened his shirt, and reached down to her. "Come." She took his hand, in its odd-to-her human form, and had the absurd thought she'd want to hold his hand anywhere, anytime, for any reason.

They had a quiet, uneventful ride to Billionaire's Row. Plutus only spoke again when he thanked the driver, as usual, and chatted casually with the doorman.

After initial pleasantries, where she learned Plutus knew all about the man's daughter's high school play and asked about it, he introduced her. "Dan, this is E Micheals. I know there is official paperwork I need to file, but informally I'll tell you she is welcome in my apartment, with or without me, at any time."

"Nice to meet you, Ms. Michaels. Of course, sir. You file the form online, but even before it goes through I'll remember her pretty face."

"The pink hair also makes me memorable, Dan," E laughed. "And please, call me E." She reached out to shake his hand.

He took her hand in his and gave it a firm, if quick, shake. She knew he wouldn't call her anything informal, for a number of reasons, but she wished he would. He was still polite and said, "Of course, miss."

"Okay, then, Dan. We'll see you again soon." Plutus clapped him on the shoulder and they moved across the vast marble entry toward the sleek elevators. When they entered, he flashed a key fob by a black reader before hitting a pretty damn high number on the panel. The elevator shot up swift and sure and Plutus mumbled, "Need to give you the extra fob."

"You don't–"

He cut her off with a look. "I will give you the extra key fob when we get in my apartment."

When the doors opened, they stepped into a foyer. "You have the whole floor."

"No," he said, stopping the elevator door and bringing her back around to look at the panel. "See. This has 52R and 52F. Make sure you hit 52F, so the front doors open. I share the floor with another apartment. No need for a whole floor when I'm not always here."

Whole floor or not, the space would be massive given the size of the building. She wandered out and Plutus let her. E moved from room to room, taking in the huge open kitchen, dining room, living room, and the tastefully decorated three bedrooms, all with their own ensuite and lovely views, the office with two desks, one clear and brand new. She wasn't about to ask about that one, so she moved back into the living room.

It was a lot, she couldn't lie. When Plutus tried to say something, she stopped him. "I need some wine."

"Not another espresso martini?" He swooped in close, taking her in his arms and cradling her so she looked up into his impossible handsome olive-skinned face. She reached up, slipped his amulet over his head, and he melted back into place, his skin taking on the gold cast, his horns flashing back into view in a blink. E even felt his claws grip where his hands held her back. She shivered at the hard press of them, of him in his true form, into her.

"You have that?" she asked, her voice husky to her own ears.

"Oh, E. I have everything you need." He dipped low, kissed her hard and long, then set her back on her own feet. But only so he could go off and make her the drink she wanted.

He was right about that, she was certain. Right then, she needed more than a drink. She needed something harder and hotter to get over her usual life stress and all the new luxury at her fingertips, making her feel uncomfortable. She stripped while he worked with his back to her over at his sleek glass and wood bar.

"I made it with a little chocolate kick, so---" Plutus jerked to a stop right after he spun around, a splash of espresso martini hitting the floor. E didn't think he cared. She sure as shit didn't care, not with her being naked and Plutus's glowing green eyes roving over every inch of her body.

Without a word, he took the few steps toward his dining room table, laying the cocktail down before he suddenly appeared in her face. He tossed her in the air and she felt weightless for a moment, until his strong arms clasped around her and brought her down so she landed with a soft oomph over his shoulder. One clawed hand rubbed before it left her for a moment, coming down with a hard, swift smack that echoed through the open space.

He moved with a deliberate, steady pace back into his apartment and she only registered some of the things she saw: extra doors, dark gray walls, a set of open double-doors they moved through, lush brown damask walls and a giant bed. She noted the last because she bounced on it one, two, three times when he tossed her down. The thing was massive, maybe even bigger than a California King.

E'd have to investigate bed size later, because the breath whooshed from her followed closely by all other thoughts as Plutus crawled up her splayed body. He looked like a big cat stalking its prey, but she wasn't afraid. She was dumb with lust and need, but never afraid with him, despite his appearance and strength and magic.

He ripped off his shirt, moved to one hip to remove his pants, then popped back over her, his heavy, hard dick grazing her belly, leaving a smear of precum there. He cocked his head at her, a question without asking, and they hovered there for a long minute.

"What are you waiting for?" It might have sounded a little bratty if she wasn't so breathless with need.

"What do you want?"

"For you to fuck me."

"Happy to oblige," he said with a wide, fanged smile before he adjusted and rammed into her waiting heat in one strong thrust.

E yelled out, not in pain but triumph, as he wound his arms around her, holding her in place by wrapping his clawed hands over her shoulders from behind. He dipped his head down, skimming a horn across the crown of her head as he breathed hot and fierce into her ear. "Hold on," he growled.

She wrapped both hands around the warm expanse of his shoulders and held tight as he started pounding into her. He adjusted a few times, until she keened as he skimmed over that perfect spot inside her. Then, focusing with the intensity of a god, he went to work, setting a relentless pace over and over the same spot, until she shook from his onslaught. "Give it to me, E. Give me what I want," he said before dipping down to take a nipple into his mouth and worry it with a long, sharp fang.

She didn't need much more encouragement. She shook, screamed his name, then she came, her pleasure a deep dive off a high cliff. As she drifted back down from the high climb and fall, she felt his pace stutter. He gave a hard shout and came inside her, shuddering.

He splayed on her, giving her all his weight. When he caught his breath, he did lean up on his elbows to stare down at her. Aftershock, and something deeper and more overwhelming, wracked her body as she lay pinned by his stare.

He noticed and bent to nudge her with his nose until she bent her neck so he could trail kisses along the scars there. When he was satisfied, he looked down at her and grinned. "So, welcome to my home."

E cackled, looping her arms around his neck, then planted a big kiss on his grinning face.

Chapter 14

Waking up in a giant, lush bed felt good to E. Or maybe it was the hard, warm arms snuggling her tight to a golden chest that had her aching to stay right where she was. Alas, she had work. E groaned at the thought of having to face Mitchel after a fabulous night, but when her alarm blared again after her snooze time ran down, she wiggled free from Plutus and plodded into the spa-like black marble bathroom connected to his bedroom.

She used the toothbrush he'd given her, jumped in the shower, and gave herself a quick scrub down. Very necessary given the sweaty activities of the night before. Thinking about it, and the delicious ache between her legs, made her groan again but in a much more fun way. Also made it harder to not crawl back into bed with the god sprawled there when she exited the steamy bathroom.

Plutus's golden skin stretched taut and sparkly in the soft morning light. His eyes, usually so bright and clear, looked sweet and sleepy. His elbows were cocked, propping his mouth-watering torso up so he could look over at her. Somehow, even hazy with sleep, the smirk still held firm on his face.

"Good morning," he said, dipping his head so his horns came up and down in a slow bob. He took his time looking her up and down as she stood slightly damp with only a towel wrapped around her.

His voice was impossibly growly. It hit her core when he said, "Could I convince you to stay in bed with me today?"

"No. Nope. No way and no how," she said. E tried, desperately, for nonchalance and firm resolve with those words, but they came out in a rushed, breathy ramble that had the god chuckling as he slipped his elbows free and plopped back down on the bed. Which managed to look graceful rather than ridiculous. He was too damn smooth for his own good. She scowled at him.

Somehow, without even looking at her, he knew and said, "Wipe the look off your face or I'll spank it off for you."

She jolted upright and scurried as if going back to the bathroom, though she stopped mid-step and changed course. She needed clothes, and hers were still rumpled somewhere in the living room. Trying to inch toward the door without getting too close to Plutus's sexy orbit, she heard a laugh ring out and watched the god roll over in his bed to pin her with an amused look.

"Plan on wearing wrinkled clothes to work?" When she didn't answer, he pointed toward a large set of double-doors along the opposite wall. "You have clothes in the closet," he said. She screwed up her face to snap something and he stopped her with an upraised hand. "Before you throw a fit, I did not buy you more clothes. I simply went to your apartment and brought back some of the clothes I already gave you. You're welcome for such a sacrifice, by the way. It's hard on me when you don't let me spoil you."

"You'll live," E threw over her shoulder as she marched into the impossibly large walk-in closet. Plutus had racks of clothes and shoes crowding half the space. The other half held a few items from her apartment. To be honest, E couldn't know for sure if they were clothes he'd already gotten her. She didn't do an inventory. He could get away with slipping new things in there, but she'd never tell him as much.

Running a hand across the dangling clothes, she took a moment to savor the feel of soft and expensive fabric on her fingertips before pushing the thought aside. Another thing she'd never admit to Plutus because he'd run with it, wearing her down until he gave her everything he could.

Why not let him?

Those four little words exploded in her head like a flash bomb. She shook off the desire and the excuses.

Work.

She had work to get to, so she randomly grabbed a crisp button-up shirt, a lush cream silk with black stitching from some French brand she'd never heard of, then spotted matching pants in the opposite design, black silk with cream stitching. Damn but silk pants seemed too ridiculous. Not at all practical. Still, they glided on her skin, slightly slippery and almost like flowing water she could wear. Despite the impracticality, she wore them.

She went through the rest of getting ready, Plutus directing her to the hair products and makeup he also had for her. When she stared at the obviously new stuff for a touch too long, he let her. E turned to him eventually, and with his now trademark smirk, he gave a shrug and admitted, "It's not unheard of for someone to have multiple beauty products, especially when they may be going back and forth from one place to another."

"I'm going back and forth now?" She asked, yanking a heavy boar-bristle brush through her pink hair. She reached for a claw clip in what appeared to be *her* drawer in his bathroom when he spun her around. Bending down, he pinned her against his hard body and the cold marble of the bathroom vanity.

"No," he growled. "Not if I can help it. But give me this."

He gave her this, that was the whole fucking point. Or sticking point. Whatever. Either way, she had no time to argue. She was about to tell him so, when he dipped lower, taking her mouth in a searing kiss. His large, oh-so-skilled claws came up to grab two-fistfuls of her hair and deepen the kiss. The slight tug, the small ache, made her core flutter in anticipation. Before it went too far, he released her, spun her around to face the mirror, and gave her a sting of a slap on her ass. She blushed at the impact, a hitch in her breath making her chest rise. He gripped her throat then, lifting her head and turning it so her cheek bloomed full on in the mirror. "Gorgeous," he growled before he released her and stepped back out of the bathroom, almost too quick for her to clock the actual movements in the mirror.

E let loose a deep but shaky breath then went to rebrush her hair and finish getting ready, rushing out of the bathroom and Plutus's apartment in a flash. She only stopped to take the offered tumbler Plutus shook at her. "You have coffee downstairs. Go."

She looked at the cup, saw a thickish, light liquid through the clear lid and took a tentative sip. Strawberry and banana smoothie. Delicious.

"You make this?"

"Told you I like to cook," he said in answer, leaning his too broad shoulders against the wall by the elevator.

"Making a smoothie isn't exactly cooking."

"Okay. I like to feed you. In whatever way I can."

It wasn't a joke. The openness of his face when he said it told her everything about the honesty of his words. Instead of replying, she reached up on tiptoes and placed a quick peck on his cheek.

He didn't say anything either, but he did give her a broad, sincere smile as he tagged the elevator button. In moments the doors dinged open and their silent searching of one another's faces came to an end.

"Have fun with all your books," he called with a jaunty wave.

She laughed. "Have fun with your godly duties." The doors closed. Oddly, she felt a little heavier when she lost sight of him.

Lucky for her, she wasn't rushing into her little work nook that morning. Doubly lucky, she didn't encounter Mitchel first thing. In passing, Brian mentioned something about a meeting with IT about database entry issues. Nothing to do with her, so she got right down to business, sticking her magnifiers on her head and continuing the meticulous task of undoing what a book binder did, centuries ago.

When she blinked up from her desk an hour and a half later, Anne stood by her desk. Her beaded glasses chain clanked slightly against her chunky beaded necklace. "Hey, E. Do you have a minute?"

E then noticed the twisting hands, the tight skin around her eyes, the darting looks around the room. "You okay, Anne?"

"Yeah. Yes. I just... Can we talk? Outside? For a second?"

Now worried, E slid her goggles off and rose from her desk, gesturing for Anne to lead the way. They walked out of the restoration section, downstairs, and into the open courtyard in silence. Visitors mingled and a few kids laughed. Anne found an empty bench away from the interior door and sat. E followed and Anne grabbed up her hand as soon as her butt hit the seat.

"I'm so sorry I talked to Mitchel about that dang missing book," she muttered.

"Huh?"

"He's been asking a lot about you, E. I think–. Gosh, I don't even really want to think it, but I do." She swallowed hard then in a rush said, "I think he thinks you took the book. Maybe that you've been taking other books, given all that's gone wrong with the database lately."

"Huh?" What else could she say? E had the book, of course, but there wasn't a damn thing she could do about it according to Plutus.

Regardless, *The Book of Desires* wasn't even in the database anymore, which might as well mean it didn't exist in this collection. Also, there were security cameras out the wazoo in the workspace. They'd clearly show she didn't go anywhere near the book. Though, she did hope there was no way it could show the book magicking itself into her bag. Something to ask Plutus about tonight.

"I think he suspects you stole the books and somehow cleared the database."

E shook her head, her thoughts sparking and firing in rapid succession, trying to think through the implications and what she might be able to do about all this. Or if she needed to do anything. Mitchel had always had a certain aloofness toward her, and now it seemed to be outright distaste. After her asking for more money, and the missing book. Money and the book. God damn it all, he likely thought she stole the book because she needed money, since it all went down on the same day.

"I didn't take anything." She didn't. It was the truth. The book found its own magical way into her bag that day.

"I don't think you did," Anne assured before biting her lip. "But, with the way Mitchel keeps bringing you up, pointing out things about you, he might believe you did. I just needed to let you know."

"Thank you for telling me, Anne." She squeezed the woman's hand and saw her shoulders slump. "You're not to blame for this, you know that, right?"

"I'm the one who isn't even sure the blasted book was there. Mitchel also only vaguely remembers something. It's all ridiculous really, but he's zeroed in on you for some reason. I can see it in his beady little eyes."

"He has been odd with me lately," E muttered then shook out her thoughts. "I didn't take your missing book, or any others for that matter. Hell, there's plenty of security cameras around to prove the fact. I'm not going to borrow worry. Neither should you."

Anne gave a fake smile and said, "Sure. Good call, E," before pulling herself free and patting E's shoulder firmly. It was a comforting gesture that might have been awkward, but E appreciated the sentiment behind it. Bookish people were often awkward even when they didn't want to be.

"Thanks again, Anne. Knowing helps. I'll keep my head down and hopefully all this will blow over soon."

Anne's round cheeks scrunched up in a grin and she gave E two thumbs up before rising. "Whelp, best get back to it."

"Yep," E called, but her mind wasn't on undoing pamphlet bindings. It was firmly on what Mitchel might have planned for her, despite knowing he had no proof she had *The Book of Desires*.

"Want to grab lunch together?" Plutus purred over the phone. Somehow, he knew exactly when she'd packed up her work for lunch and slipped from the preservation area because her phone chimed right as she stepped past the glass, card-entry-required doors.

"Can't" she said, and he gave a little *hmph* of noise on his end. He sounded as she felt: disappointed. She wanted to have lunch with the god. Not only because the eye candy was nice, but also because she wanted to talk to him. Laugh with him. Get her mind off the worry loop she told Anne she wouldn't ride.

She'd tried. She really had. But part of being an academic was being good at looking at a problem over and over and over again, trying to find a solution. The Mitchel situation was a problem, and she'd find a solution. Somehow.

Because of this, though, her work had been slower, so she needed to get back to it. No reason to give Mitchel something else to not like her over, such as missing a project deadline she herself had given him. "I'm grabbing a quick hot dog down the street, and then right back here to finish up some things before the end of the day."

"Um-hm," he said in her ear just as she stepped out of the front of the building and saw him leaned against the car. She dropped the phone from her ear, hitting the end button as he did the same. Sliding it in her fancy-pants bag, she watched his human-looking hands slide his in his pockets as he sauntered over toward her, meeting her halfway.

"Hi there," he said, the smirk on his face matching his voice.

"I really don't have time–" she started, but he took her arm and turned them toward the closest hot dog cart.

"I know. I'll just walk with you. Maybe have a hot dog myself."

The way his Adam's apple bobbed at the words made her laugh out loud. "You ever even had a hot dog?"

He looked offended. "As a matter of fact, I have. A few times. At baseball games."

"How long ago?"

"A few decades," he admitted.

She looked him up and down, not worrying about the street in front of them because he led her along. "I take it you've never had a hot dog from a cart?"

"No, I've never had the pleasure."

"Oh, it is a pleasure, Plutus."

He looked down at her and growled while also managing to lead them both around a couple who'd stopped in the middle of the sidewalk to take a selfie. "I'll show you pleasure."

"I know you will," she chirped, feeling lighter with the few minutes of banter he gave her. "But so will I." She stepped up to the cart and ordered two dogs and two sodas from the kind, older man who asked about her books like he always did. What she didn't do is let Plutus have a say in what they got, and she for sure didn't let him pay, but his narrowed eyes on her told her she'd pay for the move later. E didn't mind that at all.

"Sit," she said, directing him to a small, knee-high wall in front of a building by the cart. "Let's eat."

He stared down at the hot dog, packed with relish and mustard, gave a shrug, then took a giant bite. Chewing, his head cocked in consideration, he gave it a moment. Then he declared, "Not bad," before taking another big old bite. He scarfed down the thing in about four bites, much quicker than E'd eaten half of hers.

"Looks like it's better than 'not bad.'"

He shrugged and leaned into her. "When something's good, it's good. Doesn't matter where you found it." Inching closer, he swiped a firm thumb at the corner of her mouth before sticking it in his own and sucking it. She froze before he whispered "mustard," and she never knew a condiment could sound so sexy.

She couldn't do sexy right then, so pushed past it by taking another bite and chewing with care. Plutus moved away a few inches then started asking her about work. When she scoffed, he pressed. "What's wrong?"

"My coworker, Anne—a lovely woman by the way—thinks Mitchel suspects me of stealing *The Book of Desires*."

A sneer marred his gorgeous face. "Mitchel," he spat out, as if the name was a cuss word.

"Tell me about it," she muttered after a big swallow. "I didn't steal it, but you and I know it is at my apartment, so I'm worried what tapes might show."

"If the book came to you, it did so in a way it would not be detected."

"Are you sure?"

He scooted closer, cupped her cheek, and said, "Yes, E. I am certain of it. However, if you'd like me to do more to help- "

"No. No. If there's no proof, there's nothing he can do. They don't even have proof the book was there, so it's not like anyone would believe a book was stolen from a secure facility and erased from the database without a trace because some wily grad student wanted it. It's just an issue because we've been having issues with books being erased from the employee database, which has Mitchel's panties all in a bunch."

"If you say so," he hedged, worry creasing his forehead.

"What?"

"I don't want to worry you, E, but in my long experience, if someone with authority wants to blame someone without it of something, they will."

She twisted the now-empty hot dog foil in her grip, doubt creeping slowly and surely over her.

"Hey," he said, snagging her chin to have her look up into his eyes. "I'm here. Anything happens, we'll figure it out. Together."

Ease settled as the rope between them thumped a deep bass note. She never trusted anyone, much less men she'd just met, but she trusted Plutus to help her. Knew he would if anything happened. Which was the only reason she refocused and shoved the worry to the side.

"Right. Let's talk about something else."

"Like you allowing me to take you to a nice restaurant tonight?"

"No request to spirit me off to Paris for dinner on the Eiffel Tower?"

He pulled her up with him and led her back to the museum. "Believe me, E. If I even for a second believed you'd let me do something like that, you'd be on my jet with champagne in hand within the hour."

She snorted. "I did not need to know you have a jet."

"Of course I do. How else would I travel? I'm not Boreas."

She was about to ask how his god friend travelled but he'd led them back to her work, and they stood beside the car, the driver holding the door open for him.

"See? Only twenty minutes of your time."

She couldn't believe it'd only been twenty minutes, but digging out her phone, she saw he didn't lie. Not that he would, she knew that about him. "Thanks for the mini lunch."

He ran a hand down her cheek then gripped the back of her neck, bringing her face close to his. "Don't think I'll forget about your little move with paying for lunch."

"If you want to buy me things, you should let me buy you things."

"Touché." A pause then he added, "Still, you'll get my palm later for that one."

She shivered in his grip then laughed and pulled herself away. Only because he let her. "Stop. I have to go."

His smirk melted, replaced with a glacial look past her. E followed his gaze to see Mitchel standing there, upright and uptight, staring at them from just outside the door.

"Your boss?"

E gave a big sigh. "Sadly, yes."

"I should walk you in."

She stopped him with a palm to his hard, hot chest. Which somehow seared her hand even through his suit jacket and tie and button-down shirt. "No, you will not."

He stiffened, then took his eyes from Mitchel and trailed them down to her. He paused, huffed, and gritted his teeth. She imagined his fangs would be bared if he wasn't wearing his little magic necklace "Fine. But only for you, little one."

Before she could reply, he swept her up in his arms and gave her a quick but thorough kiss. She was half dazed when he sat her down and turned her around by her shoulders. He leaned down to whisper in her ear, "Go get him," and gave her a little shove. The push propelled her, but not awkwardly. It gave her force, a little pep in her step, as she walked away from the god.

"Mitchel," she said with a nod as she reached the man. She didn't bother looking behind her to Plutus, but she knew he was still there, as evidenced by Mitchel's stare still lingering at the curb.

"Your... friend... should not block the entryway."

"He's nowhere near the entry. He is clearly at the curb."

Mitchel looked at her, gave an open sneer, and said, "Maybe I misjudged you, Edith. Considering the value some of our books might have on the black market, I did wonder about your change in appearance. As have others, thanks to our continued book entry 'glitches.' Now seeing your friend, maybe you've come into your new-found luxuries in another way."

E gaped. He'd not only out right said he suspected her of stealing because of the little bits of wealth she now wore, he also implied she slept with Plutus for money. Mitchel was an ass, but that seemed like even more ass-ish behavior. She managed to pull herself together and rein in her anger enough to ask, "Should we continue this conversation with HR?" They'd likely do nothing, of course, but being questioned by anyone was enough to annoy a man like Mitchel.

"No need, Edith. We both have work to do. I have a book I must find."

"Then you should go find it," she bit out, stepping past him. E kept her head high, her walk steady, but she seethed inside. Her high from lunch with Plutus was now gone, thanks to the idiocy of her stick-in-the-ass boss.

Chapter 15

E avoided Mitchel for the rest of the day, though she felt his stare on her several times when he walked the restoration floor like a security guard on patrol. Or a lord hawkishly eyeing his serfs more like. However, E managed to push his grating presence aside and focus on the work she loved, the delicate pages freed by her steady hand piece by piece.

The physical work acted as a meditative activity despite all the things swirling around her: the spell book, Mitchel's doggedness about the damn book, her thesis that still needed more time and finesse to finish, whether she'd continue on to a Ph.D. or stay with her original plan to return to Columbus. With all this, Plutus also hovered. Not exactly in the periphery, because his presence even in her mind was bulky. It loomed. He was there, everywhere, connected to all these other worries in one way or another, and adding another, new worry she'd never had before, one she didn't want to articulate just yet.

Before she knew it, a hand, older with soft pink square nails, tapped on her workstation. E squinted up at Anne through her googles. She looked all packed up and ready to go. "Um, E?" The woman nodded over her shoulder, at Mitchel standing by the door. "It's a little after closing time. I stayed as long as I could, but I do need to get home to the kids. I could spare a few more minutes, if you need me here."

E eyed the antique wall clock on the far wall. Already 5:30, and she'd not even noticed the time. Anne had stayed behind for her when she didn't have to do so. It caused a lump to clog in her throat. "Thanks, Anne. Appreciate it." She cleared the croak and continued, "but unnecessary. I just finished."

Anne gave her a kind smile and patted her on the shoulder before turning to the door. E had no friends here, beyond Anne, and being here alone with Mitchel might not be a good thing. Not that the fastidious man would stoop to do anything physical to her, though he was a man, and a woman never knew. But what if he made up some story about her when there were no witnesses? Maybe a bit paranoid, but not something she wanted to deal with now that his book-stealing suspicions were loud and clear.

Anne slipped through the doors just as she finished the last gentle maneuverings to placing her finished project in its velvet storage box. Luckily, she hadn't really taken anything out of her bag during the day, so she ripped off her goggles and didn't bother unpacking her headphones or phone. E headed right for the door, Mitchel a crisply dressed sentry standing in her way. She wouldn't give him the satisfaction of backing down or acting guilty. She'd not stolen the book even if she did have it.

"The York project is completed," she said, her quick strides firm even with her short legs.

"A whole day ahead of schedule," Mitchel said, the tone in his voice saying he was in no way impressed.

"I'll be able to take up a new project tomorrow morning."

"Hhmmm," he said. "We shall see."

She breezed past him, heading for the door and only digging through her bag for her phone when she knew he could no longer watch her. She'd missed a few funny texts from Lisa who apparently had a drunken night out in London. One text from Plutus: "Dinner at my apartment." Not a question. A statement. A command from a god. Fine by her. He cooked well.

His car was waiting for her at the curb when she exited.

As she sat in the back and watched the city slide by, she thought on what she could maybe calm in her life. She had to buckle down and do her thesis work, but it would get done. There was no way to control Mitchel and what he might do, but she could get answers about the book. From the god she headed towards. Maybe those answers would also help calm some anxious energy she felt about the god in question, too.

Looked like tonight would be another round of the question game.

He cooked biryani for her. The mound of rice and meat and spices looked mouth-watering, and the smell it gave his entire apartment was inviting. Warm and comforting, like a big hug.

They'd said little to each other after she showed. Plutus kept busy in the kitchen and after she yelled out a "hello," E motored to the bathroom to wash the workday off her face then changed into a comfy but lux lounge pants and tee-shirt set she found in the monstrous closet. They looked like they were for her, so she just put them on, still thinking through what needed to be said.

When she'd sat down at the dinner table, Plutus placed the food in front of her and she forgot about questions for a moment, taking a large bite and slipping her fork free of her mouth with a moan.

"I do love the fact you appreciate my cooking, little one, but if we're to finish this meal, you need to at least attempt to not make such noises." It was a tease and a promise, the smirk on his face and heat in his eyes telling her as much.

She nodded but didn't engage, and the smirk faded. E ate several more bites, the silence between them more tense the longer it lasted.

"What's–" Plutus started to ask, but she stopped him.

"We need to play the question game."

He leaned back in his chair, eyeing her. "Need," he repeated. A statement, not a question, because he was as good at the game as she was.

"Yes. Need." She paused then gave him more, because he did deserve it. "As you know, I'm having some issues at my internship, thanks to *The Book of Desires*. I need answers to help me navigate those issues."

For some reason, Plutus stiffened and sighed, but he nodded and gestured her to continue with his hand.

"Okay. What's the origin and purpose of *The Book of Desires*?"

"Hecate created it with a human witch. A man she fell in love with, actually. After we left the human word behind, many of the gods were lonely, in need of something to help them navigate a new existence. Hecate created the book of spells to help her fellow gods find what they needed."

"What they desired."

"Exactly. What each desired most, based on the spell they cast."

"What—?"

"Uh-uh, E. Quid pro quo."

She nodded and waited, maybe a touch impatiently, as Plutus looked her over then asked, "What else happened today at work?"

She wasn't used to sharing such things with someone. It made her feel itchy inside, uncomfortable, but she'd set up the game, and she wasn't going to squirm out of it. She told Plutus about Mitchel's shitty innuendos after lunch. He cursed under his breath and took a long pull of wine before saying, "He is truly a wormy little man." E suspected Plutus might even know more about Mitchel's character than she did, given his powers, but she didn't ask. She had other, more pressing questions.

"Why did the book come to me?"

"Because of the spell I cast. I've already told you this, E." For the first time she could remember, he looked away from her. Not good.

"Have you changed your mind about wanting me to take care of Mitchel?"

"Take care of." She twisted the words around in her mouth. Taking care of things seemed to be Plutus's default setting, and one that chafed her for a variety of reasons. "No need to smite him just yet."

She expected a smirk on his face after she said it, but he looked hard, stony, a vision of how frightening an angry god could be, even when most of the time this god acted carefree and fun-loving. "Truly, Plutus. I need to 'take care' of this myself."

"In my opinion, E, you need to learn to let others take care of things for you from time to time."

She bristled. "I can take care of myself."

"Sure," he groused, stabbing into his plate and shoving a bite of delicious food in his mouth. "But I get to revisit this conversation if he continues to harass you."

E only had two questions left in their little game, but he was acting so odd about it, she knew it was important to push this. "What spell did you cast?"

Silence lasted several beats before he whispered, "I will answer this question, truthfully. Only after I ask you another. Are you certain you want to know?"

That didn't sound forbidding at all. Still, she nodded at him.

In a blink, he stood beside her, pulling her into his arms and carrying her over to the large leather couch in his living room area. He sat her down and twisted in the seat to face her. He didn't touch her again, hold her, try to do more, which was out of character. His physicality with her was an almost constant, but he gave her space in this moment.

A deep sigh then he looked her square in the face and gave the oddest answer. "I cast a spell to find my mate."

"Mate. Mate. *Mate.*" She repeated the words like she didn't understand it, but she did. On an intellectual level at least.

Mates were known to humans. Supernaturals had them, werewolf mates being the most prevalent. It made up a good chunk of supernatural romance media over the years. Mates were special. Eternal. The one person for another. "Gods have mates." She stated it as fact.

"Yes, little one. Gods can have mates, and a god's mate is a special thing. To cherish. To care for. To nurture. Godhood is lonely in its long, long existence. Mates ease the burden of time. One reason Hecate created the book. Some use it to find purpose, passion, understanding. Often, such wishes lead them to their mates regardless. I, however, didn't muck about." He gave a rueful smile. "I cast the spell to explicitly find my mate. You found the book and called me forth when you should never be able to do so."

He reached up to tuck her hair behind her ears, but E reeled, jumping up from the couch and pacing. "Mate. Mate. The thing in my gut. The drive to be with you." She muttered, lost in her own thoughts.

"Humans are not always mates for supernaturals, but it does happen. My mate happens to be a spunky, pink-haired, book-loving human." He didn't reach for her again, despite saying such things, soft blows to her understanding.

"This is... it's a lot... and there's so much." Her hands started to flutter like birds, trying to release some of the nervous energy flooding her system. She couldn't help herself. There was too damn much going on to be able to immediately process the fact she was a god's mate.

"You can trust what you feel, E. Trust me."

"Trust is earned," she whispered without looking at the god. He was right about her feelings for him, feelings that had been there from the start. But trust? Full trust? The trust one would maybe put into a mate destined by fate or something seemed suspect to her.

Plutus huffed out a sigh, his first sign of frustration with the conversation. "I believe I've done a great deal to earn your trust."

She barked out a humorless laugh. "In the week we've known each other?"

He was in her face in the next breath, close and hot and demanding every bit of her attention. "If you were being honest with yourself and not stuck in your past, you'd see what I say is true."

Her hands shook as she poked him in his chest. "See. That right there. That's why I can't fully trust you."

"I'm only telling you the truth. As I always have. As I always will. Although, I can admit that may have come out too harsh." He closed his eyes, pulled in a breath, and reached for her. E sidestepped him.

"No, Plutus. I need time. Away from you."

His face fell, realization and fear mingling.

"E," Plutus called out as she rushed to the elevator, scooping up her work bag along the way.

"Please, Plutus," she whispered, not turning back, not wanting him to see the tears threatening to fall from her eyes. "Please, let me go."

He was there. Always fucking there, in her gut and her head, but just then, he was there in reality, hot and comforting at her back even when he was the thing she needed to be comforted over right then. "I will never let you go, little one. I cannot. I will, however, give you the time and space you need right now. I'll be here, waiting for you to return to me."

She left him standing behind her as she entered the elevator and whooshed down, down, down and away from her gods-damn mate so she could think all this through.

Her anger lasted about half the drive to her place. Then she deflated into a depressed little puddle. She groaned as soon as she face-planted into her double bed in her apartment. One reason: it wasn't the comfiest to land like that. Another reason: the damn sheets smelled like smoke and whiskey and tarnished metal. They smelled of Plutus.

She'd left his apartment in a snit, not looking back at him. E suspected his face would look much like she felt, confused and hurt and maybe a little pissed off. How was she the mate to the god of wealth and luxury? She didn't know bupkus about those damn things. She knew about books and classes and study and poverty.

And now, all this stuff at her fingertips, this comfort and security she'd never known, and something in her told her not to trust it, to hold back, to make sure she was the only one she relied on. And, despite that, she'd come to rely on Plutus. Not for those material things, but for the banter and the sex, and more than anything, the general feeling he gave her. Warmth, comfort, safety. He was a big, worn blanket in a way, or he'd come to be that in her head. Then he dropped this on her.

They were mates, and he'd kept it from her.

Likely because you ran as soon as you learned about it.

She turned over and stared up at the white ceiling above her bed. Gods were real. She'd learned this less than a week ago. Now she knew they also had mates, and some of those mates could be humans, and she, a regular-degular human woman in her later-twenties, was the mate of the god of wealth. A delicious god who made her melt with his kisses and hands and other things. A god who also made her laugh and think and feel not-so-alone for the first time in ages. Maybe forever.

E rubbed her belly, the spot where she imagined the tug toward him. Not imagined, it seemed. Literally felt.

She flung an arm over her eyes and squeezed them tight. She'd been in survival mode for so long, she questioned whether she deserved any good thing that came into her life, which was why she pushed back on Plutus every step of the way. More than that, however, she didn't think herself deserving of him. She'd not earned him, and she'd had to fight and scrape for every little piece all her life. Against people like Mitchel who also saw her as lesser and always would.

Plutus never had, though. But damnit, *she* did. Her history scarred her, made her hesitant and scared to have more. Because she knew a life of having little. She didn't know a life of more. Not only more things or opportunities or respect, but more love and openness, which is what Plutus himself was after. She saw it now, with the cooking for her and caring for her and doing what she liked. Even if it only was a week, the thing tugging her toward him also told her she could trust it, trust *him*. Her head, the same thing that'd gotten her so far from the trailer park, was also a little bitch at times, and told her she hadn't earned it, so it couldn't be trusted. Couldn't possibly be real.

Damn if poverty didn't do girl's head in, even when she clawed her way out of it in some respects.

She'd left him because she'd had a knee-jerk reaction to the news she was his mate. The idea they were destined, fated, and nothing would ever change that. The reality of him being there, always, if she simply trusted it as her new reality. Still, it was so, so hard to trust in someone else.

She tucked her arm under her head and turned over, curling in on herself. E needed to work through her shit.

Obviously.

Because running out on a hot god when he told her they were mates was a dolt move. Truly. Never mind the timeframe or her past. If they were mates—and she believed they were because of what she already felt for him—then she needed to put on her big girl panties and face it. Talk it over with him. Get to the bottom of her issues. Maybe go to therapy.

While there, she might have to dig into why she revolted every time anyone tried to help her. She did it with Lisa all the time. She was doing it with Plutus. E kept everyone at arm's length, at such a distance she didn't have to take anything from people.

The problem was, there were people in her life who cared for her. Loved her. People she loved. Who she'd do anything for. For forever, it'd been okay in her mind for her to give, but never to take. E figured taking was weak, or unnecessary, even as she gave when and where she could. It was an obvious double standard she needed to work on, not just for herself, but for all the people in her life who wanted to help because they cared for her without conditions. Like Plutus.

Even then, she wanted him there to hold her, big-spoon style, as she sorted all this shit out in her own head. But she'd run away like a child. Possibly understandable given the gravity of the news he'd kept from her, but also stupid of her because he'd become the only thing that could soothe her. He was hers, *MINE* echoing in her head once again. If she felt that, she had to be his also, right? That's how mates worked, or so she thought.

Mates or no, she liked him. Cared for him. Thought of him when they were apart and enjoyed all the time they spent together, sexy and otherwise. "Bittersweet," she whispered to herself, harkening back to their MOMA date, his one word like an arrow in her chest. The one word that summed up her feelings for that painting and about life in general in many ways. The way she didn't feel about Plutus. Sure, he frustrated and annoyed her, but more often she felt cherished. They laughed and teased. They talked books and art and random things. They pushed one another in productive ways. She wanted all of that. Needed it, in fact. Needed him, if the ache in her chest meant anything.

Well, shit. She loved him already. She'd have to deal with that, along with her running, shortly. Sitting up in her bed, she thought about calling him for a split second, but decided against it. He'd come in all his godly speed, she knew for certain. But she wanted to also give him space. Maybe she also wanted to lick her own wounds. Or give herself space after acting like a petulant teenager before she pulled up her britches and apologized.

Maybe she'd hold off the love confessions for later, though. He deserved to know, and she deserved to tell him, but at the right time.

Chapter 16

The car was outside her apartment. E was thankful because she'd had a sleepless night kicking herself. She hoped Plutus waited in the car for her, but she knew better. He'd have been waiting outside the thing, propped up against it with his insolent lean and smirk. Or looking worried about her reaction. No way he'd have waited inside the back of the car for her to climb inside.

The driver shut the door after her, and she found a piping hot, velvety cappuccino waiting for her. Plutus was there in spirit, taking care of her. Always taking care of her, even if it'd only been one week. Now, she knew, he was looking out for his mate.

Nope. She shook her head hard to dislodge the word. She couldn't think on it then. She'd spent the night chewing it over, coming to the conclusion it not only felt right, but somehow made her feel better about all the luxury and care around her. If she were his mate, it made sense he shared and protected. It made sense for her to trust it. Made even more sense when she was honest with herself about trusting him from the jump for some reason. A reason tied tight to the rope around her middle that tugged whenever he was near. The mate bond. Everything seemed so much more logical, and easier to accept, with the mate info. She just needed to swallow her pride and go talk to Plutus about it. However, she had to work, and face Mitchel, first.

When she exited the car, the driver stopped her with a soft, "Miss?"

"Huh?"

"Whatever he did, he's sorry."

"He told you to say this?"

"No, but he's a good, fair boss. I saw it this morning when he gave me your drink and told me to come get you and not worry about him."

She nodded to him in thanks, patting him on his arm for his words. "I know. So am I. It'll be fine."

The man looked relieved, and she wondered why he was so invested, but didn't dwell. He asked if she needed a ride for lunch, but she told him no. She'd have a new project and she'd just eat something quick from the little cafe in the museum section. She didn't do it often because she couldn't always afford it.

Now she could.

Her badge wasn't working properly. She pressed it to the little black box outside the glass door to the work area a few times, the red light flashing after every pass. Anne strolled in and slid hers over it to let them both in. "Tech, right?" she said with a little grin. "Guess the database issues are now extending to security."

"Yep. It's why I like books so much. They're more dependable."

"Ain't that the truth." Anne gave a small wave as they split apart and went to their separate workstations.

E opened her work tablet, but it didn't take her password. She set the thing down, looking around the room to see if anyone else had issues. Everyone appeared to be starting their workday smoothly.

"Edith," Mitchell called, his voice cold and clipped. "Problems?"

"Yeah. Um, it looks like I'm having tech issues. My badge didn't work earlier, and now I can't sign in to the database to get my next project."

"You were not assigned a new project." He didn't even bother to look at her, instead focusing on the gleaming cufflinks in the crisp white shirt under his suit jacket.

"Why?"

"You'll find out soon enough," he said, turning hard on his heels like a military cadet and stalking toward the door. "You may want to check your university email if you haven't done so today."

Dread sat heavy in her stomach as she plopped down in her chair and pulled her phone from her bag. She clicked the email app, scrolled past the few random listserv emails, and found what Mitchel somehow knew was there: a new message from her academic advisor asking E to meet with her in her office at noon, with an assurance she did not need to go to work today.

Mitchel knew something was up, maybe even made something be up, but she couldn't think on it too much, or she might hurl all over her workstation. That would not make her look good. She sat there, stunned, then mind racing, for a solid twenty minutes before she slipped her phone back in her bag.

"E, you okay?" Anne called from somewhere, but the voice sounded far away, like the room suddenly became cavernous. E waved her off and, head down, moved out of the workspace, out of the work wing of the museum, out of the museum, without much thought.

E couldn't hide the hard jerk of her head when she walked into Dr. Hamilton's office to find Mitchel already seated, ankle resting on his knee, a bland smile on his face.

"Edith." He practically purred, but she ignored him and looked to her advisor, who seemed to be trying hard not to look up at her as she shuffled through papers at her desk.

"Ms. Michaels. Please, take a seat."

She perched on the edge of the seat, gripping her bag to herself like a shield instead of setting it down beside the chair. "Why am I here?"

Dr. Hamilton sighed and finally looked up at her, her bespeckled eyes filled with enough pity to make E swallow the sudden surge of extra saliva in her mouth. "Your mentor for your required internship has brought a number of concerning accusations to me."

"Accusations, not proof." E wasn't backing down in this.

"Only because you somehow manipulated the evidence," he said back coolly, as if it didn't matter to him. As if he wasn't trying to ruin her career before it even started.

"There is no need for additional recriminations, sir," her advisor said, a bite in her voice making E hope she'd take her side against the man. "However, such accusations are concerning and could cast a long shadow over our entire program, not just you, Ms. Michaels."

The dread returned, swift and powerful. "They are still only accusations."

"True, which is why the three of us are having a conversation instead of a meeting with the graduate director and chair of the department. Or, worse, the board overseeing academic integrity."

E gritted her teeth. This shit was serious, and even if he didn't have proof, just being accused in a wider forum could put a black mark on her record she might never be able to remove.

"What are the accusations?"

"That you stole books from the library and digitally erased the evidence of your theft."

"I did not steal any books." She spoke the truth. The one missing book she had any knowledge of went with her willingly. Found her, actually, because of Plutus using it previously. Because of the fact she was Plutus's mate. None of this was his fault, however. It all rested on the toad with the slimy smile seated next to her.

"The latest book, if verified, would have been a particular boon for our collection. A rare find, as you well know, Dr. Hamilton, a spell book intact. Witches do not part with such history easily." E snorted at his words. Of course witches didn't part with their spell books easily. In fact, the few human museums and special collections where spell books were held acquired them through the usual human means: death and destruction for gain and conformity.

He cut eyes to her but continued his story. "One of our full-time employees was given charge of the tome then discovered it missing. An outright theft, unlike the more subtle thievery of the previous books."

E glowered but bit back at him. "You're certain the previous books are missing? Before, you assured everyone it was just a technical glitch in the system."

He ignored her question and went right on with his so-called evidence. "In the following days, Edith showed to work looking like...*this*." "He flung his hand in her direction.

"Excuse me?" she asked, with far more bite than she might normally show in front of an advisor and boss.

"Come, Edith. The same day the spell book went missing you asked for a raise. You said you asked the department for financial relief as well, yes?"

Dr. Hamilton nodded in confirmation before E could reply.

"Next workday, you show up with Burberry accessories, Louboutin shoes, new clothes. Suspicious to say the least."

Dr. Hamilton also nodded, and E looked at her bug-eyed.

"You're going to believe this asshole's take?"

"Ms. Michaels," her advisor snapped back, as if the most atrocious thing of the day was E cursing and raising her voice. Not that this dude was trying to drag her down.

"Whether or not you believe me, I did not take the spell book in question or any book for that matter. Also, you have zero proof I took any books. If you had any, you wouldn't be talking to her. You'd have called the cops." He was the type to call the cops at the smallest thing, so he for sure would've had cops busting down her door if he could.

He scowled at her, and she gave him a sharp smile in return, now sure he in fact tried that move first and they told him to get lost.

Dr. Hamilton held up a hand, and looked over E as the silence stretched. "If you assert you did not steal from the collection, and Mr. Collins has no proof, there is little I can do." Mitchel cleared his throat, leaned forward, ready to argue, when she then stopped him with the same hand. "However, I cannot have such accusations tarnishing the good name of this department. Therefore, here's the compromise I propose. Ms. Michaels, you will stop working at the museum immediately. I've spoken with your committee and they all agreed to meet for your defense in two weeks. You will present your work then, rather than at the end of July, and be evaluated accordingly. If you pass, you will graduate in August as planned, but you will no longer be affiliated with this department in any way." The offer of the PhD program was off the table, then. E didn't care too much about that at the moment. She was too busy internally freaking out over the fact she had only two weeks to finish something she thought she had six weeks to complete. That's a whole lot of work to cram into a very short time.

"I don't see how–" Mitchel began, but Dr. Hamilton spoke over him.

"Unless you can provide actual proof of her misdeeds, sir, you have no grounds to ask for more."

He stood and adjusted his coat in jerky movements as he sneered down at both women. "Good day," he said to the room, stomping out in a man huff.

"Ms. Michaels," her advisor began, her voice much softer than before now that Mitchel was gone, but it was E's turn to halt her words with her hand.

"There is no proof."

"No, but academia is a small world, and accusations take root quickly. They'd smear you, and by extension me, if a scandal broke."

And there it was. Dr. Hamilton was saving herself at E's expense.

She huffed out a laugh. "I guess I should count myself lucky you'll let me graduate. If I can finish in time."

"I also won't pull my recommendation for the Ohio State job."

"Thanks," E said, her word dripping in sarcasm.

"This is an ugly matter, and I'm doing what seems fair."

"Fair to you, maybe, but not fair to me. Though people like me don't often find fairness and equity in academia, right?"

"Now, Ms. Michaels."

E stood, ready to be out of her presence, done listening to her in any way. "Never mind. I have to go. Lots of work to do. I'll see you in two weeks."

She scurried out of the office and her advisor didn't try to stop her. Her heart felt heavy, constricted, like she'd have a panic attack at any second.

She wanted Plutus.

Chapter 17

As soon as the elevator doors slid open and E faced Plutus's apartment, he was there in front of her. Like he'd been waiting outside the elevator doors since she called him.

He didn't worry about his own feelings. Didn't rehash the big argument they'd had only the night before. Plutus took one look at her and asked, "What's wrong?"

She knew she had to look devastated, because she felt it in her bones. The devastation of being helpless in a system designed to work against her in so many ways. "Fuck 'em," she muttered, her mind still racing.

"Fuck who, little one? Who needs to be fucked. Not me, right? Or, at least, not in the way you said just now. In a different, far more pleasurable way, I hope."

She did manage a laugh. He wasn't trying to make her laugh, either. Worry etched his beautiful golden face. His horns tipped down toward her as his chin buried itself in his hard chest so he could study her, figure out what went wrong. Help her. She knew he'd help her.

"Mitchel and my advisor are the people to whom I was referring." She was so stiff, so formal, for no reason. Until she melted at a soft touch on her shoulder from her mate. Her stiff back and locked knees finally gave way.

Plutus caught her, of course, pulling her tight against his chest before twirling her around and half carrying her to the couch, where he sat her on his lap like a ventriloquist dummy. She blinked up at him and he shoved a stray pink hair off her forehead and tucked it securely behind her ear. "Please, my E. Tell me what happened?"

It wasn't a demand, but a question, and she knew he'd never demand anything from her. Unless they were in bed. He wanted her to give herself, her life, to him. Not force her to reveal herself. Not strong-arm trust from her. He was sneaky, cheeky, pushy at times, but never forceful with her. The least she could do was give the info he wanted right them. She blurted it all out in a rush. Without pause. Maybe without breathing or blinking, she couldn't really tell.

A growl grew from Plutus's chest with each detail. It started low, a hum almost, but rumbled higher and higher until the final word. Which might have been because her voice broke a little at the end and she visibly swallowed down the tears threatening to claw their way free. She just couldn't cry. Not then. Gods, she had too much to do to sleep, much less lose herself in tears.

She did have the time to lay a hand on his warm chest, uncovered in his favorite home attire of a Grecian robe. The growl vibrated, a force against her hand, as she looked up into the green eyes she often saw filled with humor. They were cocked in cold calculation just then. Until he blinked rapidly, shook his head, and cleared his own throat, so he could speak.

"What's your plan?"

"To prove them all wrong. To show them I can do whatever I need to do to succeed. Without being a bitch about it or sabotaging others. I'm going to do the damn thing, even if it means two weeks of sleepless nights. It will get done."

Plutus gave a solemn nod, as if he expected nothing less from her. "What do you need from me, E: quiet support, solutions, or vengeance?"

She wanted to damn the god for making her teary-eyed with the question. Simple enough thing on its face, but they loudly signaled the man he was, the way he could push his initial reaction away to give her what she needed and wanted.

She knew he'd do the same, repeatedly, the rest of her life. If she'd let him. And in that moment she felt even more foolish about running out on him the other night.

Reaching up to caress his cheek, she watched, fascinated, as his clenched jaw flexed then smoothed at her touch. A laugh slipped out at the idea this powerful god seemed to be putty in her hands, molten gold willing to form in whatever shape she needed. She only needed his true shape, though, and she knew it with even more certainty after this little episode.

"Quiet support. With the addition of tasty food to fuel my long days. However, I reserve the right to call for mighty, godly vengeance later."

"May I give the man a small taste of my wrath?"

"How small?"

"Nothing to mortally wound or maim, but enough to teach him a lesson he desperately needs?"

She didn't want any smiting to happen on her account, but something smaller didn't seem too off course for the jackass. E nodded, and a wide, wicked smile lit Plutus's lips.

"Now, little one. Do you need any of your research materials from your apartment or do you have what you need with you? I can go get whatever you require. I'm also mid-roast so you'll have work fuel soon enough. I'll leave details of the tiny smidge of vengeance for later, as a little treat for getting all your work completed. Which I am fully confident you will do, in spectacular fashion."

During his little spiel, he set her off his lap and rose from the couch, ready to do whatever she required. Ready to give her whatever she needed in this moment of crisis. He towered over her, like he did the first night she met him when he'd crowded her against the exposed brick in her apartment, claws clamping on her neck and massive fangs exposed in a snarl. She remembered the look, but for the life of her, she couldn't imagine it now. Not from this god. Not from her mate. Her love.

In absurd fashion, much like her life of late, she just blurted it out then, without preamble or forethought. "I love you." It wasn't a whisper, but a solid statement with weight and certainty.

"Oh, little one. My love." He scooped her up for the second time in half an hour, smooshing her tight to him as she hovered off the ground. He pulled his head back while still holding her close to his warm, somehow purring, chest. "You are my mate. Beyond that, you are the funniest, smartest, toughest woman I've known in my long life. We are forever connected as mates, but I must say, fate chose well. Because even if you were not my mate, I wouldn't be able to help loving you fiercely."

Those tears threatening to fall broke free, but for a good reason. She gave him her heart without thought, but if she'd thought about it, she would have fully expected this. The acceptance of all she was with all he was. He looked concerned then, wiping away her tears. "E? Are you okay? I apologize if–"

"Oh, kiss me, you silly god," she said around a tear-filled laugh.

He wasted no time fulfilling her request, and she knew her life would always be this, from this moment forward. If he chose to stay with her, go with her. Because she couldn't be in New York City anymore.

That final worry had to be pushed to the side, however. They could talk about it later. When she finished her thesis and defended the hell out of it. When he wasn't kissing her with a hot, needy passion she wanted to meet.

He picked her up and she followed, wrapping her legs around his hips as they continued to kiss deep. Plutus carried them back to his bedroom with ease and laid her down gently in the middle of his bed, following her down but catching himself on his elbows so their lips finally broke apart.

One clawed hand came up and stroked her from forehead to chin before his forehead dipped down to meet hers. "There's so much I feel, so much I want to say…"

"Sshhhh," she said, moving to kiss his cheek. "The feelings are good enough. Words can come later."

He pulled up, a bright smile on his lips, then gave her a kiss on the nose before he moved down her body, tossing every scrap of clothes she wore when he got to it. Soon enough, she was naked before him, his mouth and tongue leaving hot trails up her legs until they hit her pussy. She quivered as he paused there then cried out in bliss as his tensile tongue licked over her clit in gentle sweeps. He nuzzled, licked, and sucked softly until she was a writhing mess. "Please," she said between pants.

He moved up her body in answer, pausing only to roll to her side so he could undress at lightning speed.

"You have no need to beg, my E. No need for anything ever again."

He nudged her legs apart with his own, dropping between her open thighs and hiking her knees up and over his hips. Then, he slid home, and she moaned loudly at the stretch and rub of him.

He moved with deliberate, controlled motions, the ebb and flow never increasing or decreasing, until the steadiness of it became almost too much for her to bear. But she'd bear it, because he wanted her to. Because he knew what her body needed, always. Because she loved him and loved the way he made her body feel with his own.

Her pleasure climbed higher and higher, moving up a ladder until a rung snapped and she toppled fast and hard, crying out in Plutus's ear as she did. He waited there to catch her, whispering "My love, my E," as she calmed.

Only then did he keep moving, his pace more insistent as he chased not her pleasure but his own. She cooed to him, encouraged him, called him hers, as he found his own pleasure deep inside her.

His sweaty brow hit hers once again and she breathed deep the tarnished metal and smoky whiskey scent of him, loving the fact she also had that smell lingering on her now. They kissed, sweet and languid, before he moved off to her side and simply held her until she needed to take care of herself. Then he held her as they both rested, despite the other shit that'd happened to her that day. With Plutus by her side, she could make it through. She knew that, just as she knew she loved her mate.

Chapter 18

She camped out at Jefferson Market Library from open to close for the next two weeks. On day two, she felt a tap on her shoulder around noon. She took out her headphones and turned in her chair to find Anne with a sad smile on her face, wringing her hands.

"Hi, E."

"Hey, Anne. What are you doing here? Why aren't you at work?"

"It's my lunch break," she said, her hands fluttering about like caged birds. "I'm here to say I'm sorry. So, so sorry."

"Oh, Anne," E said, needing to somehow calm the older woman. She stood and hugged her, letting the embrace warm her, hearten her, a little more. She moved them away from her table and into a dark, quiet hallway so they could talk without disturbing others.

"This isn't your fault."

"You don't have a job now, and Mitchel bragged about catching the thief in our midst, when I know you didn't steal anything. Couldn't have."

"Really, truly, fuck that guy," E bit out before she focused back on Anne. "He made accusations to my academic advisor, which means if I want to graduate I have to get my thesis done in about one-third of the time I originally had to finish it all up."

Her shocked gasp said it all. Anne had her own graduate degree, so she understood the amount of work it took.

"Don't worry. I'm going to graduate if I have to be sleepless for two weeks. I'll use every minute I have and get it done. Because I need to, and because screw him."

Anne gave a weak laugh, but it was a laugh. "I came to say I'm sorry, and I did. Now tell me how I can help."

"What?" E blinked at her. Plutus was helping in his own way, as she knew he would. He was helping her relax, feeding her, making sure all the daily life things went smoothly so she could focus on getting the data synthesized then finish her writing. She didn't even consider asking for help from other people in her field. Hell, she hadn't even told Lisa what happened.

Shit, she would be pissed when she found out.

E added that on her mental to-do list then looked back at Anne. She'd had her little epiphany about letting other people help her. It was time to put aside her fear of pity and focus on the good people she managed to have in her life, because she sure as shit could use the help right then. "You want to see what I'm doing? I don't exactly know if there's anything you can help with, but if you look it over, maybe you can think of something?"

Anne beamed at her. She adjusted her glasses on her nose and said, "Let's do this."

Anne pulled up a chair. They whispered together, and in about fifteen minutes, Anne had E sending her all the finished chapters for review. "I might not be able to do the writing, but I sure can edit. Send me the first draft of your final chapter when it's finished and I'll get it back to you in a jiff."

"Thanks, Anne."

"Anytime," she chirped before she rose to go. E waved goodbye and as the woman walked away, she thought about how she'd maybe missed out on so much by not asking for help before. She did the work, always would, but having a helping hand now and then wouldn't hurt her. It also wouldn't mean she didn't do it. This summer she'd learned: she shouldn't always go it alone.

Heaving a big sigh, she turned and hunched back over her laptop. She'd worry about her posture later. Rubbing her eyes, she also thought she'd sleep when she was dead.

"That utter and complete fuckwit!" Lisa yelled into the phone. E left the library early, deciding to work at Plutus's apartment for the rest of the evening so she could take the time to call her best friend.

"I know. Gods, he's the absolute worst. Don't ever, ever work for him."

"Noted. But, also, how are we getting even? Need me to hop on a plane and meet him in a back alley with a baseball bat?"

"Lisa! Little bloodthirsty, aren't you?"

"Hey, I am a New Yorker born and raised. You don't mess with my friends."

E's heart squeezed at the truth in her words. "You're the best, Lisa."

"I know. So are you. Which is why we work."

"I miss you."

"Samesies."

E swallowed then moved on to the other big topic. "Also, uh, you should know. I met someone."

"Oh, do tell."

Right then they pulled into Plutus's garage, and she saw the god waiting there for her. "He's pretty awesome."

"Hopefully pretty, too," Lisa quipped.

"Oh, yeah," she breathed as Plutus opened the door.

"How are you this afternoon, little one?" Plutus asked as he took her hand to help her out of the car.

"Is that him?!?!?! Damn, that voice is enough to make me squirm. Good on you, girl. London is dead. Or maybe I'm dead from all this work."

"I hope you get to meet him," E said and Plutus smirked at her as he led her to the elevator, now very aware she was talking about him.

"I hope he talks dirty to you with that voice."

"Oh, I do," he purred. Of course he could hear Lisa through the headphones.

"Hey, Lees, I have to go. Got lots more work to do."

"How can I help?"

"Will you double-check my numbers?" It still felt weird, asking for the help, but she did need it.

"No problem. Email me access to your data set, and I'll run it through my software. Make sure everything is good on your end."

"Thanks, friend," E whispered.

"Any time, E. Every time. Now take a little break and go be with your deep-voiced mystery man. Later!"

"Byeee!" E called out before she heard the two deep tones meaning the call ended.

"Lisa?" Plutus asked as they stepped into the elevator.

"Yeah. She's going to help double-check my numbers. Anne came by the library, too."

"Anne?"

"Yeah. I mentioned her before, I think? She works, sorry worked, at the museum with me and was the one Mitchel gave *The Book of Desires* to before it bolted. A bit out of nowhere, but she came to apologize for how things went."

"Not her fault," Plutus groused, and the deep set of his brows told her he was thinking of Mitchel.

"True. I told her as much. She also offered to help by editing my finished chapters, which is a godsend."

"I thought I was a godsend?" He enveloped her in his arms.

"I mean figuratively for Anne. You're literally a godsend. Or just a god. Don't know how that one works."

"As Hecate made the book, I suppose she sent me to you in a roundabout way."

"Is she still around?"

The elevator opened into his apartment and he led her inside as he answered. "Yes. Somewhere. I help her with investments from time to time but haven't spoken to her in several years. Why?"

"Just thought I might need to send her a fruit basket or something."

"The book caused you a great deal of trouble, E."

"Yes, but it brought me you, so I wouldn't change it."

Plutus planted himself firmly and quickly so E bumped right into him. He whipped off his medallion, melting into the monster she loved right before her eyes.

"I wouldn't change anything either, little one."

"I know. You were super grumpy when we met, so I figure you were miserable before I cast that spell."

He snorted. "You didn't cast the spell. I did."

"Tomato. Toe-ma-toe."

Another snort. "Whatever you say, little one."

Before she could reply, he lifted her high in the air and she landed with an oomph across his shoulder. "Hey! I have work to do."

She managed to dangle her bag down and lay it gently on the living room floor before he stalked toward the bedroom. He bent her over the bed, her toes barely reaching the floor, and Plutus landed a hard smack on her ass and she yelped. He leaned over her, draping her in his scent and his weight. "You need an orgasm. Maybe two. Then dinner. Then you can work all night long."

"Who am I to argue with a god?" She asked, her voice dipping low with the sudden rush of lust coursing through her veins.

"Remember that next time," he said, the bite of bossiness in his voice making her squirm in his hold. She heard the rustle of clothes, felt the wet nudge of him at the small slice of skin where her cropped shirt rode up and her jeans held tight thanks to the fancy leather belt he'd bought her.

Adjusting a smidge, he ground into her ass, hitting right at her cleft and giving her the most delicious friction. His hands moved over her sides from under her shirt, snaking into her bra from the bottom and scraping claws gently to and fro across her nipples. When she tried to push back, he rose up, pulled one heavy hand free from her bra, and shoved hard down in the middle of her back. Then his weight was back, and his breath hot in her ear, as he said. "Stay right there until I tell you you can move."

She might have squirmed, but she didn't try to do much more. His hands roamed, amping up her need, until he took his arm off her back and undid her jeans, gliding them down her body until they, and her panties, circled her ankles. She felt him move behind her, notch himself at her wet heat, then slowly push into her, inch by delicious inch.

He sat there, balls deep, for several moments. "Fuck me, little one." He stood there, firm and sure, as she just managed to push her ass back so she slid down the length of him, feeling every etch and rib of his golden cock as she did. She dug her toes in, moving her hips back toward the bed so she got the luscious exit slide of him.

Plutus didn't help or hinder her, as she fucked herself on him as best she could. Still, she didn't have a great deal of leverage and couldn't give herself what she really needed. "Please, Plutus. Please." She began to whine.

"Does my little one need more, hhmmm?"

"Yes. God yes."

He scooped up her hair in a fist and leaned down when she notched herself against his hips once again. "I'm the only god you call to, so say my name next time, love."

She nodded, but rocked in an instant when he slid out of her then slammed back home. He set a punishing pace, forcing her to claw at the sheets and groan incoherently in an almost embarrassingly short amount of time. She didn't care though, because she loved every second. Plutus loved every second, too, she knew, thanks to tightening mate tie humming between them.

E clenched, shuddered, and screamed out her release, letting some of her stress and worry go along with her orgasm. Plutus followed soon after her, planting himself deep and leaning back over her.

Once they'd caught their breath, the god pulled out and spun her around, taking a moment to gently pull her panties and jeans back in place. His clawed hand snapped her button closed with a definitive click of metal on metal and she laughed. "Not going to clean me up first?"

"Nope," he popped as he moved to pull up his own pants. "I like the idea of you sitting in me for the rest of the night."

"Ugh. No thank you. Too wet. And too dangerous. I'm not getting a UTI because of you, thankyouverymuch."

"Then clean yourself up," he called out to her as he exited the bedroom, a teasing smile on his lips.

She snorted. If she asked, he'd clean her from head to toe. She knew that for a damn fact. With a soft chuckle to herself, she vowed to make him do that one day. Today, though, she had more work to do, and now, some clean up duties.

Chapter 19

Plutus went with her to her defense. He couldn't be stopped, god that he was, so she didn't try.

Honestly, she didn't want to try. He comforted her, so she was glad for some quiet time with him in the car. His hand on hers helped give her mind something physical to focus on instead of the anxiety of what was about to happen. She was about to walk into a room with three people, all set to judge her.

She'd done all she could. Finished her thesis with three days to spare, just enough time to give her committee the opportunity to read through it. E felt proud she'd met the deadline, all things considered. She'd be even prouder if she passed the damn defense. *When*. When she passed the defense.

She became fidgety the closer they came to the department, and the only thing that broke her out of her own head was the deep growl erupting from Plutus when they eased in front of the building. She looked at where he stared outside the car and saw Mitchel slinking there.

"What the hell's he doing here?"

"I don't know, but I'm about to find out," Plutus's voice was an anvil, a mountain, anything cold and hard and immovable.

She imagined his claws and fangs would be flashing if he wasn't wearing his amulet just then.

However, he looked cool, calm, and steady as he exited, stared down the other man, and helped her out of the car. All at once. How's that for multitasking?

"May I help you?" How Plutus managed to make his voice have the exact note of richness and dismissiveness was impressive to E.

"I'm here to speak with her," Mitchel spat out, and she noticed he looked a little less put together than normal. His suit hung limply and wrinkled, and his eyes looked a little puffier than usual. His hair wasn't slicked back, but mussed in a not-attractive way.

"Not. Happening." Plutus clipped at him, placing himself a step ahead of her, almost like he had the night with the vampire. E snorted, because Mitchel was a vampire of sorts, though not a cool or interesting one.

"She got to the board." His voice cracked halfway through the yelled accusation, but E simply blinked at him.

"I have no idea what you're talking about, Mitchel."

"Liar! Thief!"

"She's being honest. I'm the one who spoke with the board. Had a lunch meeting with three members. John, Carlton, and Francis to be specific. Hadn't seen them in ages."

E cocked her head at Plutus, thinking he knew an awful lot of board members and he'd never brought that up.

"You? Why? What lies did you tell them?" Mitchel demanded, stepping close to Plutus.

"Bad move," E muttered under her breath as Plutus straightened further somehow, towering over the man before him in a menacing and not at all sexy way. Well, not at all sexy for Mitchel, most likely. Sexy as hell for her in the moment because he was putting Mitchel in his place. Admittedly, she liked whenever he loomed, menacingly or not.

"I told no lies, Mitchel Collins. I had no need when you have transgressions of your own. Including, but not limited to, your baseless accusations against E."

"They are not baseless. She had to have stolen the book. Or seduced you into–"

Plutus's hand shot out, gripping the much smaller man by his lapels and leaning down, inches from his face. "Be very careful what you say next." The grit and menace of his voice was loud and clear.

Mitchel managed to squirm free, but E figured it was only because Plutus let him. He rubbed his hands together, as if rubbing away grime, and continued. "You also had some recent discrepancies in your database, not just with the missing book you accused E of stealing. Discrepancies which pointed to more than one stolen book that happened to make their way to backroom dealers with money to spend. I figure you wanted someone to pin all those dealings on, no?"

Mitchel's mouth opened and closed like a hooked fish. The weird "glitches" in the databases that disappeared books. Mitchel's hyper focus on one book, and her. It made so much more sense now. "You lousy, conniving jackass," E called, surging forward to get in his face. Maybe even take a swing. You can take the girl out of the trailer park and all that.

"Whoa, little one. No need for more. Mitchel is simply upset about the consequences of his own actions. What was it again? Ah, yes. Administrative leave, without pay, effective immediately. Hard, isn't it, when your old money is dwindling daily thanks to a string of truly stupid investment decisions."

"How would you know?"

Plutus' green eyes flashed. "Why else would you resort to stealing from your employer?"

"I never–"

Plutus waved a hand at him. Pure dismissal, as if he were beneath the both of us. Which he was, the toad. "You should run along. You might find authorities at your door soon enough, as there was evidence against you. Unlike with E. Also, I suggest you check your digital payment methods soon: debit cards, touchless pay, etc. They seem to be on the fritz of late."

A wide, wicked smile stretched Plutus's mouth and Mitchel huffed. Because he was who he was, and he never had to learn self-preservation, he spun to throw some more vileness at E. "You'll regret this. I will end–"

"Enough!" Plutus pushed the man back, step by step, until Mitchel was shoved against the brick building. He crowded him and E only heard what he said to the man because she was right on his heels. "The only reason you stand here now is because of her mercy. You will never interact with, look at, think of E again, or you will find yourself in a much more dire situation." Mitchel cried out in pain and E noticed Plutus had a finger poking right into his chest. Hard. So hard he might leave a bruise. "It is past time for you to run along."

Mitchel gave her one last hard look over Plutus's shoulder but did as he was told. Likely off to figure out how much trouble he was actually in.

"Is he going to jail?"

"Most likely. Unlike you, he did steal and there is a trail. He was a careless idiot about it." Plutus spun around, straightened his suit jacket, and smiled down at E. "No more of him. Ever. He will pay for what he did to you and his general jackassery without any more from us."

"The vengeance of a god," she whispered up at him as she gripped his freshly straightened lapels.

"Watch the suit," he said, his tone telling her he didn't care a bit about his suit.

"Watch the lips," she said before she stretched up on her tiptoes and smacked a quick, hard kiss on him. "Thank you."

"You never need thank me for a kiss, love," he said with a smirk.

"I kissed you, dude. And not for that. For doling out justice."

"All in a day's work," he said, with a little salute. He kissed her again, this time making it deep and on the edge of wicked. "Now, go wow your committee, as I know you will."

"Will do," she said, stepping away, a little more bounce in her step thanks to what Plutus did for her and to her.

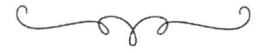

E waited in the hallway like a chump.

It was an odd thing, to have three professors pepper you with complex questions for two hours then ask you to wait in the hallway, while you knew they were in there talking about you. Lucky for her, it only lasted about five minutes, though it felt like five hours in her hazy mind. She was running on adrenaline and massive amounts of coffee at this point. She couldn't remember the questions they'd asked her. It all existed in some half-panicked daze even through it was literally minutes ago.

"Ms. Michaels. Please come in," her advisor called from the doorway. E entered the ordinary meeting room to her other committee members standing. "Congratulations. You've passed your thesis defense with no revisions."

There was clapping, a few pleasantries, talk of the ceremony in August, which E knew she wouldn't attend. She didn't say as much then, of course. She'd email her advisor about it later. For now, it was enough to take the congratulations and leave as quickly as she could so she could get to the person she really wanted to celebrate with.

She exited the building expecting to see Plutus waiting there for her. The car sat there of course, but no Plutus. She slumped in disappointment but the driver beamed at her. "He's waiting for you at the apartment with a surprise, Miss."

"Told you. It's E."

"Master E?"

"Yep."

"Nicely done," he said and she reached out to shake his hand.

"Thanks. Now I'll collapse in the back until we get home."

He smiled and nodded, holding the door open for her so she could crawl in and decompress for the length of an uptown ride.

She was done. Done. No PhD for her, especially not here and now. Maybe one day. Who knew? After the messed-up sendoff she had, she was finished. Not finished with books or academia fully, because she'd still take the job at OSU, but finished with degrees and NYC for now.

The last thought shot a bolt of panic through her. Would Plutus be willing to come with her to Columbus? Could they do long distance if he stayed? The idea of leaving him behind made her ache, but she couldn't stay here. She'd never be comfortable as a lady who lunches, though she knew Plutus would happily give her such a life. They needed to have a talk about it, she knew, but damn. She'd just done something major. She deserved to celebrate a little. Which she'd do with Plutus as soon as she saw him. They'd discuss the future later.

She rested her eyes all the way back and fidgeted in the elevator until it pinged open. Darting out, she started teasing right away. "You better have a damn good excuse for not being there when I got out because I wanted to tell you that I passed. Your driver was the first to know."

"We were second. He texted before he started back," Plutus said, a huge smile on his beautiful, human face. Odd to see in his own home. He stepped aside then, not coming to hug me like usual, because my parents stood right behind him, tears in their eyes.

"Mom? Dad?" The world turned watery at the sight of them.

"Oh, baby girl. Congratulations. We knew you'd do it." Her mom barely got through that before the tears fell.

"Way to go, baby," her dad whispered, then they barreled into her, and all three cried happy tears together.

When they managed to disentangle themselves, she turned to plant her face square in Plutus's chest. "Thank you."

"You're welcome, E."

"You got a good man, there, E. Very kind. Called us last week with this plan and all. Got us the tickets and a hotel and everything. Plus, we're going out somewhere fancy to celebrate." Her mom blabbed in her endearing way, and E saw she was half in love with her god, too, given all he'd done.

"Busy."

"Had to be, what with you so consumed with work for the last few weeks. Needed something to occupy my time." He smirked down at her.

"We're going for steak tonight," her dad chimed in. Offered steak would be at the forefront of his mind.

"Where?"

"Delmonico's" Plutus said, as if it didn't shoot an arrow straight through her chest, the idea that he remembered her talking about going there with Lisa and her family, how special the experience was to her. His face softened and he added, "I rented out the bar area for the night. Also, just so you don't get too teary-eyed in front of others there, know that Anne and her husband and Lisa and her parents are also invited."

"You flew in Lisa?"

"I was going to, but she'd already planned on it herself."

"I'm sure she did." She thought of something that happened only weeks ago, though with the frantic pace of her life lately, it felt like it happened months or years in the past. Back to the night she first met her god. "Um, honey? There is probably still a big handprint on her wall."

She didn't say more, like how it was a giant, godly claw print pounded into the brick wall of Lisa's living room after Plutus first appeared to her. What her parents didn't know wouldn't hurt them, especially when it came to gods living amongst humans. Too much for her to deal with on an already packed day. Lisa deserved an unmarred wall, though, so she hoped they could get that fixed soon.

Plutus waved his human-looking hand and said, "Taken care of, little one."

Of course it was. He took care of everything. Most of all her.

Her mom, ignoring the entire conversation she just had and the gooey eyes she sent to her god, took E's arm and headed to the couch. "Come now, honey. Tell us all about how your test went."

They sat there, chatting and laughing, until it was time for fancy steak in the financial district, then more time chatting and laughing with friends. Actually celebrating her accomplishments for once, thanks to the god by her side.

Chapter 20

Once again, she woke up smothered by Plutus. In a good way, of course, but it made her think about how often it'd happened in the extremely brief time they'd known one another. They were mates. They'd admitted they loved one another. All in the span of less than a month. What they had yet to do was talk in concrete ways about the future.

"I can hear you thinking," Plutus said. The words were seriously muffled because his face was firmly planted in his sheets.

"Thinking's not a bad thing."

"No, but maybe you need a break from it." He jacked up, spun around, and held her tight to his chest. An exaggerated sigh left him. "I guess I will have to help you with this as well."

"You are so helpful," she said, as his hand moved to grab hard to her naked ass. They'd stumbled into bed mostly undressed the night before, but far too drunk to do much but kiss and grope before they passed out. However, it was morning. They had a little time before she had to meet her parents for a tourist day, and very little clothing or sheets, separated her slick core from the growing hardness she felt against her stomach.

"Always," he said, bending down to give her a long, languid kiss that stole her breath.

They were in no rush. Both let their hands roam the others body, sometimes stumbling over one another in their need to keep contact. Only after long kisses, hard grasps and a few well-placed grinds, did Plutus reach between them to test her pussy with one clawed finger. "Fuck. You feel ready, love."

"More than ready."

She wrapped her arms around him as he gripped himself and slid inside her. A sigh of pleasure and relief escaped as he started sliding in and out of her in a steady, slow rhythm. They didn't say much, just felt what they could of each other. They kissed, bit, and stroked as he moved in and out, in and out, so that it was almost a surprise when E felt her orgasm about to topple over like a stack of books. She tumbled, a jumbled mess of words and sounds and clenching need. Plutus did the same, at the same time, his own words of love and need and want mixed all up with hers.

She lay after, spent, while Plutus brought out a rag and cleaned her up. He moved her only to place her firmly on his chest and say "Rest" in his sexy, demanding voice. Who was she to argue?

She grumbled, annoyed Plutus dared to move beneath her when her sweaty cheek lay plastered to his golden chest. "Stop," she whined, though it came out distorted and she had to admit he might not have heard it. She did the only thing she could do; she jackknifed off his chest to give him the death stare of all death stares. Never mind he recently fucked her clean into his comfy mattress. She wasn't putting up with him disrupting the rest she deserved.

His smirk was planted firmly in place when she managed to brush away her pink strands. "Problem, love?"

"I was comfortable." She went for disgruntled, but it came out petulant at best.

"Poor baby," he said, his voice dropping deep and now she was wide awake from the tingle it sparked in her core. "Apologies, little one, but I have something to show you."

He turned his torso to the bedside table, tapping awake an iPad resting there. He did the tippetty-tap thing for a minute, the glow of the screen making his molten skin look more silver than gold where it flashed. Finally, he said, "Come, E," as he opened his arm. She didn't hesitate to curl into the crook of his shoulder, facing the iPad to see what he pulled up.

He didn't say anything, and E was left a little confused. It was pictures of a house. A beautiful brick house, two stories, with hard peaks jutting out here and there, black shutters and a black door, enclosed by a brick fence with old-timey looking lanterns at the entrance of the gate and to the right of the front door.

Plutus flipped through images of the house: a small foyer and open living room with cream and brick accents, a quaint kitchen with high-end appliances and more brick, a large dining room, three nondescript bedrooms, and two lush, white-marbled bathrooms.

Her voice shook when she spoke after seeing the last image, a clear view of a park she knew. One in the German Village neighborhood of Columbus. "Plutus?"

His voice lifted, soft but firm. "E. I love you. I wish to be with you. Always. You are my mate. My only. But a deal is a deal, and our bargain ends in a week. This house? I purchased it for you. You can go live there by yourself and I will fulfill my end of the deal. You will never want for anything. You will live comfortably all your days. If you wish, you can do so there while I stay away. It will rip me to shreds, but I will honor your wishes. Or I can come with you. Be with you, in Columbus."

"Do you want to leave all this?"

"Hear me, E," Plutus growled, cupping her cheek firm and training his flaring green eyes on her. "The only thing in this world I'd be sorry to leave behind would be you, and the only thing that could make me do so would be you."

"Then, yes, Plutus. Please. Come be with me in Columbus."

He snapped the cover she hadn't even noticed over the iPad and carelessly flung it back on the bedside table, where it skidded awfully close to the edge.

"Hey. You should be more careful," she said, but then she let out a little yelp when she was flipped to her back and he loomed over her.

"Live a little, E," he said between peppered kisses on her cheeks and forehead. "An iPad can be replaced."

Plutus's hand snaked under the mountain of pillows behind her head and came up with a distinct, robin-egg blue box. "However, you really should be careful how you roll around on top of this." He tsked at her as she stared.

Again, all she could say was "Plutus?" Like all her brains went out the window.

He opened the lid and a gorgeous, too-large, square-cut diamond ring sat there, nestled in delicate cream fabric. "E, you are my mate, which is enough in my world. You silly humans like your pomp and circumstance, though, so I have to ask. Will you marry me?"

E didn't answer with words. She shoved up, toppling the surprised god backward. He didn't have time to right himself as she scrambled up his long, hard body, landing with a slight oomph across his chest. She laid a long, hard kiss on him, and he was more than content to let her. When she pulled up a fraction of an inch to look up into his eyes, she saw humor and love there. Something she knew would be there with him, for the rest of her days. She was so happy she made a drunken magical mistake. Or drunkenly stumbled into a magical lottery. Whatever. The damned *Book of Desires* wasn't damned after all. It blew up her life, sure, but helped it fall into a new, lovely mess she would have fun putting together with Plutus.

"Yes," she finally said.

He laughed, flipped her so he was on top once again, and smiled as he gave her a swift smack of his lips. "Thank the heavens. You left me waiting long enough."

"Seconds," she said, teasing in her tone as she trailed her fingers up through his black hair and the length of one of his curved horns.

"Three weeks," he corrected. "Forever, actually, but who's counting, since you're here now."

She was right where she belonged: comfortable and secure in a life she made for herself in some ways, but one she let others help her create. Which, she'd learned fairly recently, was the best kind of life one could have.

Thanks so much for reading *Greedy Little Thing*! Please take a moment to rate/review it on Goodreads or wherever you purchased this book.

Want More?

Want to see who the *Book of Desires* goes after next? Join Sonya's newsletter! You'll get awesome travel and cat pics plus first looks at all her books (and any freebies she might have in the works). Find out more over on Substack (@sonyalawsonwrites).

For news and the occasional laugh, follow Sonya Lawson on social media. She's @sonyalawson on TikTok, Instagram, Facebook, and Threads.

Get all new book notifications by following her author profiles on Goodreads and BookBub, too.

You can find all things Sonya Lawson on her website (sonyalawson.com).

And, once again, please take a moment to rate/review *Greedy Little Thing* on Goodreads and/or wherever you purchased this book. All honest reviews are greatly appreciated!

About the Author

Sonya Lawson is a recovering academic who now writes romance (in a wide variety of sub-genres). Her work offers a glimpse into different yet familiar worlds that are sometimes dark, sometimes dramatic, sometimes a bit funny, and always steamy.

While she remains a rural Kentuckian at heart, she currently lives in the Pacific Northwest. Her days are often filled with writing, editing, reading, and walking old forests.

You can keep up with all her happenings by following her on social media via @sonyalawsonwrites (TikTok, Instagram, Facebook, or Threads). If you join her Substack newsletter, you'll also get early access to news and hot deals.

Acknowledgements

I always have so many to thank, so here we go.

Dayna Hart of Hart to Heart Edits aced the edits here. Gisele (@lifebygisa on Insta in case you want to see more) did this book cover, just like the last book in this series. Once again, she gave me everything I needed. Both are exceptionally talented and diligent professionals who deserve all the praise and thanks.

My monster romance ARC Team is slowly but surely growing, and I'm so thankful for everyone who joined up and gave their honest feedback on this little book.

Kenzie Kelly was, as always, the best beta reader a writer can get. Amber also gave me a great beta read with awesome suggestions and just the right amount of encouragement. Both were stellar in all ways.

As always, my friends and family pull me through when writing (or regular) days get dark. Thanks for the constant, unwavering support, loves.

Before I go, I have to say this was an emotional book in ways I didn't foresee. I grew up in poverty and a lot of my past (and my past hang ups created because of it) came out in this book. At the same time, writing a librarian character now is an inherently political choice. A person who wishes to spend their life preserving books would have many negative things to say about the state of education and book banning in America today. If any of this resonated, hugs and good vibes to you, always. You have all my love.

Made in United States
Troutdale, OR
04/03/2025